T0000394

A GIRL'S STORY
ANNIE ERNAUX

**Translated by
Alison L. Strayer**

SEVEN STORIES PRESS
New York · Oakland · London

Seven Stories Press
140 Watts Street
New York, NY 10013
www.sevenstories.com

Library of Congress Cataloging-in-Publication Data

Names: Ernaux, Annie, 1940- author.
Title: A girl's story / Annie Ernaux ; translated by Alison Strayer.
Other titles: Mémoire de fille. English
Identifiers: LCCN 2019049327 (print) | LCCN 2019049328 (ebook) | ISBN 9781609809515 (paperback) | ISBN 9781609809522 (ebook)
Subjects: LCSH: Ernaux, Annie, 1940- | Authors, French--20th century--Biography. | Authors, French--21st century--Biography.
Classification: LCC PQ2665.R67 Z46 2019 (print) | LCC PQ2665.R67 (ebook) | DDC 843/.914--dc23
LC record available at https://lccn.loc.gov/2019049327
LC ebook record available at https://lccn.loc.gov/2019049328

This work received support from the French Ministry of Foreign Affairs and the Cultural Services of the French Embassy in the United States through their publishing assistance program.

College professors and high school and middle school teachers may order free examination copies of Seven Stories Press titles. To order, fax on school letterhead to (212) 226-1411 or visit www.sevenstories.com.

Printed in the United States of America

9 8 7 6 5 4 3 2

I know it sounds absurd
Please tell me who I am.

—Supertramp

"One thing more," she said. "I'm not ashamed of anything I've done. There's nothing to be ashamed of in loving a person and saying so."

It was not true. The shame of her surrender, her letter, her unrequited love would go on gnawing, burning, till the end of her life. [. . .]

After all, it did not seem to hurt much: certainly not more than could be borne in secret, without a sign. It had all been experience, and that was a salutary thing. You might write a book now, and make him one of the characters; or take up music seriously; or kill yourself.

—Rosamond Lehmann,
from *Dusty Answer*

There are beings who are overwhelmed by the reality of others, their way of speaking, of crossing their legs, of lighting a cigarette. They become mired in the presence of others. One day, or rather one night, they are swept away inside the desire and the will of a single Other. Everything they believed about themselves vanishes. They dissolve and watch a reflection of themselves act, obey, swept into a course of events unknown. They trail behind the will of the Other, which is always one step ahead. They never catch up.

There is no submission, no consent, only the stupe-faction of the real. All one can do is repeat "This can't be happening to me" or "It is me this is happening to," but in the event, "me" is no longer, has already changed. All that remains is the Other, master of the situation, of every gesture and the moment to follow, which only he foresees.

Then the Other goes away. You have ceased to interest him. He abandons you with the real, for example a stained pair of underwear. All he cares about is his own time now, and you are alone with your habit of obeying, already hard to shake: alone in a time bereft of a master.

And then it is child's play for others to get around you, leap into the emptiness you are, and you refuse them nothing—you barely feel their presence. You wait for the Master to grace you with his touch, if only one more time. One night he does, with the absolute supremacy you've begged him for with all your being. The next day he is gone, but little does it matter. The hope of seeing him again has become your reason for living, for putting on your clothes, improving your mind, and passing your exams. He'll be back, and this time you'll be worthy, more than worthy, of him. He'll be dazzled by the change in your beauty, your knowledge and self-assurance, compared to those of the indistinct creature you were before.

Everything you do is for the Master you have secretly chosen for yourself. But as you work to improve your self-worth, imperceptibly, inexorably, you leave him behind. You realize where folly has taken you, and never want to see him again. You swear to forget the whole thing and speak of it to no one.

It was a summer with no distinguishing meteorological features, the summer of de Gaulle's return, the new franc and the new Republic, of Pelé, soccer world champion, of Charly Gaul, winner of the Tour de France, and Dalida's "Histoire d'un amour."

A summer as immense as they all are until one is twenty-five, when they shrink into short summers that flit by more and more quickly, their order blurred in memory until all that remains are the ones that cause a sensation, the summers of drought and blazing heat.

The summer of 1958.

As in previous summers, a small percentage of young people, the most affluent, departed with their parents for the French Riviera, while others from the same group, schooled at lycées or the private college of Saint-Jean-Baptiste-de-la-Salle, took the boat from Dieppe to perfect their stammering English, studied for six years straight from the manual, but hardly spoken. Yet another group—schoolteachers, lycée and university students, possessed of long vacations and a little money—went off to look after children at holiday camps located all over France, in mansions, even in castles. Wherever they went, girls packed a supply of disposable sanitary towels and wondered with mingled fear and desire if this would be the summer they'd sleep with a boy for the first time.

That summer, too, thousands of servicemen left France to restore order in Algeria. Many had never been away from home before. In dozens of letters, they wrote about the heat, the djebel,* the douars—tent villages—and the illiterate Arabs, who after one hundred years of occupation still did not speak French. They sent photos of themselves in shorts, grinning with friends in a dry and rocky landscape. They looked like Boy Scouts on an expedition, almost as if they were on holiday. The girls asked the boys no questions, as if the "engagements" and "ambushes" reported in the papers and on the radio involved others. They thought it was normal for the boys to perform their duty, and (as rumor had it) that they availed themselves of tethered goats to assuage their physical needs.

They came back on furlough, brought necklaces, hands of Fatima, copper trays, and then left again. They sang *Le jour où*

---

* In the Middle East and North Africa, a mountain, hill, or range of hills (also jebel). The location of numerous battles during the Algerian War, hence the references, in French, to "the veterans of the djebel," or "the generation of the djebels."

la quille viendra* to the tune of Gilbert Bécaud's "Le jour où la pluie viendra." Finally, they did return to their homes all over France and were forced to make other friends, virgins of war who had not been to the bled and never referred to fellaghas or *crouillats.*** Out of step with their surroundings, incapable of speech, they did not know if what they had done was good or bad, or whether they should feel pride or shame.

There are no photos of her from the summer of 1958.

Not even one of her eighteenth birthday, which she celebrated at the camp, the youngest of all the counselors. Because it was her day off, she'd had time to go into town for bottles of sparkling wine, ladyfingers and Chamonix orange biscuits, but only a handful of people had stopped by her room for a drink and a snack, and quickly disappeared. Perhaps she was already considered unfit company or simply uninteresting, having brought neither records nor a phonograph to camp.

Of all the people she saw each day at the camp at S, in the Orne, in the summer of '58, does anyone remember that girl? Probably not.

---

* A song about the end of military service, meaning "One day we'll be discharged (for good)."
** *Crouillat, crouille*: Here, a racist term for the Arabs of North Africa. Derived from the Arabic word for "my brother," *khuya*.

They forgot her as they forgot each other when they disbanded at the end of September, returned to their lycées, teachers colleges, nursing and PE schools, or joined the squad in Algeria, most of them content to have spent their holidays in a manner both financially and morally rewarding by taking care of children. But she, no doubt, was forgotten more quickly, like an anomaly, a breach of common sense, a form of chaos or absurdity, something laughable it would be ridiculous to tax their memories with. She is absent from their memories of the summer of '58, which today may be reduced to blurry silhouettes in a formless setting, or to the painting *Negroes Fighting in a Cellar at Night*, their favorite joke of the summer, along with *Closed Today* ("I passed the theater and saw a sign for a new play, called Closed Today").

She has vanished from their consciousness, the intertwined perceptions of the others who were there that summer in the Orne. Vanished from the minds of those who assessed acts and behaviors, the seductive power of bodies, of her body; those who judged and rejected her, shrugged their shoulders or rolled their eyes when someone said her name, itself the object of a pun invented by a boy who strutted about repeating, Annie what does your body say, *Annie qu'est-ce que ton corps dit?* (Annie Cordy the singer, ha ha!).

Permanently forgotten by the others, who have melted into French society (or society someplace else), married, divorced, or single, retired, grandparents with gray or tinted hair. Beyond recognition.

I too wanted to forget that girl. Really forget her, that is, stop yearning to write about her. Stop thinking that I have to write about this girl and her desire and madness, her idiocy and pride, her hunger and her blood that ceased to flow. I have never managed to do so.

There were always references to her in my journal—"the girl of S," "the girl of '58." For the last twenty years, I have jotted "'58" among my other book ideas. It is the perpetually missing piece, always postponed. The unqualifiable hole.

I have never gotten beyond a few pages, except for one year when the calendar precisely coincided with that of 1958. On Saturday, August 16, 2003, I began: "Saturday, August 16, 1958. I bought jeans for 5,000 francs from Marie-Claude, who paid 10,000 at Elda in Rouen, and a sleeveless jersey with blue and white horizontal stripes. It is the last time I will have my body." I worked every day, writing quickly and trying to make the date of writing match the corresponding date in 1958, the details of which I recorded pell-mell, as they came to me. It was as if this uninterrupted, daily anniversary writing were the kind best suited to purging the interval of forty-five years, as if this "day-for-day" approach gave me access to that summer in a way as simple and direct as walking from one room to the next.

Very soon I fell behind in my recording of the facts. The stream of words and images ran riot, branching off in all directions. I was unable to seal time from the summer of '58 into my 2003 diary—it constantly burst the sluices. The further I advanced, the more I felt that I was not really writing. I could plainly see that these pages of inventory would have to change form, but how exactly I did not know. Nor did I try to find out. Deep down, I remained steeped in the pleasure of unwrapping memory after memory. I refused the pain of form. After fifty pages, I stopped.

Over ten years have passed, eleven summers that raise to fifty-five the number of years that have elapsed since the summer of '58, with wars, revolutions, and explosions at nuclear power stations, all in the process of being forgotten.

The time that lies ahead of me grows shorter. There will inevitably be a last book, as there is always a last lover, a last spring, but no sign by which to know them. I am haunted by the idea that I could die without ever having written about "the girl of '58," as I very soon began to call her. Someday there will be no one left to remember. What that girl and no other experienced will remain unexplained, will have been lived for no reason.

No other writing project seems to me as—I wouldn't say luminous, or new, and certainly not joyful, but vital: it allows me to rise above time. The thought of "just enjoying life" is unbearable. Every moment lived without a writing project resembles the last.

To think I am the only one to remember, which I believe to be the case, enchants me. As if I were endowed with a sovereign power, a clear superiority over the others who were there in the summer of '58, bequeathed by the shame I felt about my desires, my insane dreams in the streets of Rouen, my blood that ceased to flow at eighteen, as if I were an old woman. I am endowed by shame's vast memory, more detailed and implacable than any other, a gift unique to shame.

I realize that the object of the above is to sweep away anything that holds me back, stands in my way, and keeps me from progressing, like something in a bad dream. A way to neutralize the shock of beginning, of taking the plunge, as I am about to do, and reunite with the girl of '58 and the others, put them back where they were in the summer of a year when 1914 was more recent than 1958 is in relation to today.

I look at the black-and-white ID photo, glued inside the academic performance booklet issued by the Saint-Michel d'Yvetot convent school for the *baccalauréat* in classics, Section C. The face, in three-quarter profile, is of smooth contours, a straight nose, slightly prominent cheekbones, a high forehead partially covered (possibly in order to reduce its height, though the effect is a little odd) by frizzy bangs on one side and a kiss curl on the other.

The rest of the dark brown hair is pulled up and back into a bun. There is just a hint of a smile, which could be described as gentle, or sad, or both. A dark sweater with a mandarin collar and raglan sleeves creates the austere and flattering effect of a cassock. All in all, a pretty girl with bad hair, who emanates a sort of gentleness (or is it indolence?), and who, today, we might say looks "older than her age," which is seventeen.

The longer I gaze at the girl in the photo, the more it seems that she is looking at me. Is this girl me? Am I her? For me to be her, I would have to

be able to solve a physics problem and a quadratic equation in math

read the whole novel published in an insert in *Bonnes Soirées* magazine each week

dream of going to a real party—a *sur-pat**—at last!

support the continuation of French Algeria

feel my mother's gray eyes follow me everywhere

not yet have read Beauvoir, Proust, Virginia Woolf, or etc.

be called Annie Duchesne.

Of course, I would also need to be oblivious to what the future holds, to the events of the summer of '58, and to

---

* In use until the late fifties-early sixties: teen slang, short for *surprise-partie*. Soon evolved into *surboum* and *boum*.

develop instant and total amnesia with regard to my own history and that of the world.

The girl in the picture is not me, but neither is she a fictional creation. There is no one else in the world I know in such vast and inexhaustible detail, which allows me to assert, for example, that

to have her ID photo taken, she went to the photographer's studio on the Place de la Mairie with her great friend Odile, one afternoon during the February break

the corkscrew curls on her forehead are produced by rollers she pins into her hair at night, and the softness of her gaze is the result of myopia—she has removed her glasses with their jam-jar lenses

at the left corner of her mouth is a claw-shaped scar, invisible in the photo, the result of falling on a bottle shard at age three

her sweater is from Delhoume, a dry goods wholesaler in Fécamp that supplies her mother's shop with socks, school supplies, cologne, etc., whose traveling salesman appears twice a year with cases of samples he unpacks on one of the café tables, always the same fat salesman in a suit and tie who got her hackles up the day he remarked that she had the same name as the popular songstress Annie Cordy, who sings "La fille du cow-boy."

And so on, ad infinitum.

No one besides this girl so thoroughly fills my memory. And I have no other memory but hers with which to represent the world of the fifties, the men in duffel coats and Basque berets, the front-wheel drives, the song "Étoile des neiges," the crime of Father Uruffe, Fausto Coppi and the Claude Luter Orchestra, with which to see things and people in the light of their original reality, the reality of then. The girl in the picture is a stranger who imparted her memory to me.

Yet I cannot say I have nothing in common with her now, or with the person she will become the following summer, judging from the violent distress I felt on reading *The Beautiful Summer* by Cesare Pavese and Rosamond Lehmann's *Dusty Answer*, and on seeing the following films, whose titles I felt the need to list before starting to write:

> *Wanda, Love Is My Profession, Sue Lost in Manhattan, Girl with a Suitcase*, and *After Lucia*, which I just saw last week.

When I watch these films, it's as if I were abducted by the girl on the screen and were no longer the woman I am today but the girl from the summer of '58. She overtakes me, stops the flow of my breath, and for a moment makes me feel I no longer exist beyond the screen.

This girl of 1958, who from a distance of fifty years is able to resurface and set off an inner collapse, must have a hidden, indomitable presence inside me. If the real is that which acts, produces effects, as in the dictionary definition, this girl is not me but is real inside me—a kind of *real presence*.

That being the case, am I to dissolve the girl of '58 and the woman of 2014 into a single "I"? Or proceed in a way that is, if not the most precise (a subjective evaluation), certainly the most adventurous, which is to say, to dissociate the former from the latter through the use of "she" and "I," in order to go as far as possible in my presentation of the facts and deeds. And go about it in the cruelest possible way: in the manner of people we hear talking about us through a door, referring to us as *she* or *he*, which makes us feel we are dying on the spot.

Even without a photo, I can see her, Annie Duchesne, step off the train at S in the early afternoon of August 14. Her hair is in a high French twist. She wears a navy blue car coat—her beige wool loden from two years before, cut shorter and dyed—and a pencil skirt in thick tweed—also resized—with a striped sailor jersey. She carries a gray suitcase, bought new six years earlier for a trip to Lourdes with her father, never used since, and a blue-and-white plastic bucket bag, bought the week before at the market in Yvetot.

The rain that lashed the windows of their compartment throughout the trip has stopped and the sun has come out. She is too warm in her loden coat and thick winter skirt. I see a middle-class girl from the provinces, tall and robust, of bookish appearance, in handmade clothes of durable, good-quality fabrics.

Next to her I see the shorter, squarer form of a woman in her fifties, whom one could describe as "respectable," in a skirt suit, permed auburn hair, head held high with an air of authority. I see my mother, her expression a mixture of anxiety, suspicion, and discontent, her habitual air of a mother "keeping an eye out for trouble."

I know what the girl is feeling at this moment, what she desires more than anything is for her mother to make herself scarce, get back on the train, and disappear home. She seethes with shame and resentment at being seen with her mother, who has refused to let her travel alone (so she says) on account of a train change in Rouen. She resents being brought to camp like a little kid, when in just two weeks she turns eighteen and has been hired as a camp counselor.

I see but do not hear her. There exists no recording of my voice of 1958, and the words we ourselves speak are transcribed by memory unvoiced. Impossible to say if I still spoke with a drawling Norman cadence, the accent I must have thought myself rid of, in comparison with my forebears.

What can I say about this girl, who, just before the driver for the camp pulls up to the station, rushes toward the vehicle, kissing her mother on the fly to thwart her obvious intent to follow? Leaves her standing on the pavement with a look of chagrin on her face rubbed bare of powder by the hours of travel, and the girl could not care less. Nor does she care when told of the night the mother spent in a Caen hotel for lack of an evening train to Rouen. She no doubt feels it serves her mother right: all she'd had to do was let her travel to S alone.

What, then, can we say about the girl that captures her just as she was on that August afternoon, beneath the shifting skies of the Orne, oblivious to what will forever be behind her in just three days? The girl as she was at that inconsequential moment, lost to time for over fifty years.

What can we say, not as an explanation (or not *only* an explanation) of what will come to pass and may not have come to pass had she not removed her glasses and unpinned her hair so it tumbled loose over her shoulders, though actions such as these are quite predictable, at a safe remove from maternal supervision?

What spontaneously comes to mind is: She is all desire and pride. And: She is waiting to fall madly in love.

I feel I want to stop here, as if all that has just been said is all one needs to know in preparation for what comes next—romantic illusion, a fitting description for a heroine of fiction. But we need to push on, define the terrain— social, familial, and sexual—which fostered that desire, that pride and waiting, at that point in time; seek the reasons for the pride and the sources of the dream.

Say: It is her first time away from her parents. She has never left her burrow.
Except for the bus trip to Lourdes with her father when she was twelve, and the ritual day at Lisieux each summer when, after the morning devotions at the Carmel and the

basilica, the bus deposits the pilgrims on the beach at Trou-
ville, her life since childhood has unfolded in the space
between the parents' shop and the Saint-Michel boarding
school (run by nuns), according to a fixed trajectory which,
as a non-boarding pupil, she repeats twice a day. During
the holidays, she remains in Yvetot, reading in the garden
or in her room.

As an only child, she is overprotected, having been born
after a first girl who died at six, and nearly died herself from
tetanus at five. The outside world, while not entirely barred
to her, is an object of fear for her father and of suspicion for
her mother. She cannot go out unless accompanied by an
older cousin or a classmate. Three months earlier, she danced
for the first time at the carnival ball in a tent on Place des
Belges while her mother kept watch from her chair.

To list her social inadequacies would be interminable.
She does not know how to make a telephone call, has never
taken a shower or bath. She has no experience of environ-
ments other than her own, which is Catholic and working
class, of peasant origin. From this distance in time, with her
great insecurity about her social graces and use of language,
she appears to me gauche, ill at ease, even rough-spoken.
The most intense part of her life is the time she spends
immersed in the books she has insatiably consumed ever
since she learned to read. All she knows about the world
she has learned from these, and from women's magazines.

At home, the grocery woman's girl—as she is called by the people of the neighborhood—enjoys full rights to the territory. She dips into the sweets jars and biscuit tins to her heart's content, reads in bed until noon on holidays, never sets the table and never shines her shoes. She lives and behaves like a queen.

Or with the pride of a queen, which comes less from her being at the top of her class—the natural order of things, in a sense—or from having been declared "the glory of the convent school" by the headmistress Sœur Marie de l'Eucharistie, than from the fact that she studies mathematics, Latin, English, writes essays on literature, all of these things no one around her has any idea about. Her pride comes from being "the exception," and being recognized as such by the rest of her kin, workers who at holiday meals wonder "where she gets it from," this "gift" of learning.

Pride based on her difference from others, as evidenced by habits that include:

listening to Brassens and the Golden Gate
Quartet on her phonograph instead of Gloria
Lasso and Yvette Horner

reading *The Flowers of Evil* instead of *Nous Deux*
magazine

keeping a journal, transcribing poems and
quotes from writers

doubting the existence of God, though she
never misses Mass and takes communion on all
religious holidays, which probably situates her

in the "undecided" category, a middle ground
between belief and unbelief, where the ballast
of legend grows lighter while the attachment to
prayer, the rituals of the Mass and the sacraments,
holds fast.

She takes pride in her desires, as of a special right she is
granted on account of her difference:
>to leave Yvetot, escape the watchful gaze of her
>mother, the school, the town, and do what she
>wants: read all night, dress in black like Juliette
>Gréco, hang about the student cafés, and dance at
>La Cahotte, rue Beauvoisine in Rouen
>to penetrate an unknown world made both
>desirable and daunting by signals exchanged
>between the more affluent students at the
>convent school, a world of Bach LPs, libraries,
>subscriptions to *Realités* magazine, tennis, chess,
>theater, and bathrooms, all of which prohibit her
>from inviting these students "in the know" to her
>home, where there is no living or dining room,
>just a tiny kitchen squeezed between the café and
>the shop, and the toilets are in the yard. People
>in this world, she imagines, talk endlessly about
>poetry and literature, the meaning of life and
>freedom, as in *The Age of Reason*, Sartre's novel that
>she inhabited for all of July, transformed into the
>character of Ivich.

She has no defined self, but "selves" who pass from one book to another.

I know her to possess a bold certainty about her own intelligence, and the power displayed by her height of five foot seven, her well-built body, all buttocks and thighs. She is possessed of an abstract faith in her future, which she pictures as a great red staircase like the one in the painting by Chaim Soutine, a reproduction of which she cut from the pages of the magazine *Lectures pour Tous*.

I picture her arriving at the camp like a filly that has just fled the paddock, alone and free for the first time, a little fearful. Eager to meet her peers, or those she imagines to be her peers, who might recognize her as their peer.

Her mother has always kept her away from boys, as from Satan in person. The girl has dreamed about them constantly since the age of thirteen but does not know how to talk to them. She sees girls in Yvetot, idling in the streets and talking to boys, and wonders how they do it. Only a few months ago for the first time she kissed a boy, from the agricultural school, pursuing the fling wordlessly—the boy did not talk either—at the cost of one thousand and one strategies for eluding her mother's surveillance: missing three-quarters of the mass, claiming endless waits at the dentist's office, etc. She ended things with him just before the *bac*, fearing some kind of obscure punishment.

She has never seen or touched a man's sex.

(A memory that indicates the extent of her ignorance: a girl in her class, snickering, points to a quote from Paul Claudel in the Catholic appointment diary provided by the school: "There is no other happiness for a man than to give fully of himself." Where was the obscenity in that? she wondered.

She is dying to make love, but only out of love. She knows the passage in *Les Misérables* about Cosette and Marius's first night together word for word: "An angel stands on the threshold of wedding nights, smiling, with a finger on his lip; the soul becomes contemplative before this sanctuary in which love is celebrated."

How is one to possibly retrieve all the images, fantasies, and thoughts about sex that drifted around inside that self that is just about to enter the summer camp at S?

How to resuscitate the absolute ignorance and anticipation of what is considered the most unknown and wondrous thing in life—the secret of secrets, passed around in whispers starting in childhood but never described or shown by anyone, anywhere? The mysterious act that grants us entry into the feast of life, its very essence—please God, don't let me die before—fraught with prohibition and a terrible fear of consequences in those Ogino years—the worst, in a sense, with their shimmering promise of "freedom" each month in the eight days leading up to one's period.

My memory fails to restore the state of mind produced

by that mixture of desire and prohibition, the anticipation of a sacred experience combined with the terror of "losing my virginity." The meaning of that expression, its staggering power, is lost inside of me and the greater part of the French population.

I have still not stepped through the portico of the camp. I am making no progress in my attempt to capture the girl of '58. It is as if I wanted to "build her profile" as meticulously as possible, adding never-ending "psychological and social determinants," too many brushstrokes to the portrait, thus rendering it illegible, whereas I could summarize with: "good student from a religious school in the provinces, raised in a modest home, aspires to an intellectual, bourgeois-bohemian lifestyle." Or, to adopt the language of magazines, "a girl raised in an environment empowering to her self-esteem," or, another variant, "a girl whose healthy narcissism has been allowed free rein." I do not know if the girl in the car on her way to camp would have recognized herself in these descriptions. They certainly do not reflect the way she expresses or thinks of herself, though the words of Sartre and Camus on freedom and revolt may. What I know is that at this moment, her stomach is in knots. She has never taken care of children and was accepted by the camp without having received any instruction, as she is not yet eighteen, the minimum age for enrollment in the training course.

Though I am unable to retrieve the girl's language, all the languages that make up her private discourse—which there is no point in trying to reconstitute, much as I believed it possible at the time of writing my novel *Ce qu'ils disent ou rien*—I can at least take samples from letters to a close friend who had left the school a year before, letters she returned to me in 2010. They all begin *My dearest Marie-Claude* or *Darling*, and ended with *Bye-bye* or *Ciao*, the foreign tags then in vogue among lycée girls. In the letters from the months before she leaves for the camp in S, the girl writes:

"I can't wait to leave this hole [the convent school] where you die of cold, boredom, and suffocation," and "this horrible town of Yvetot."

"To get a rise out of the good sisters, I do my hair in braids, paint my nails, and wear my school smock without a belt."

"It's fabulous to be young! I'm in no hurry to clap on the shackles of marriage."

The girl of '58 is effusive about all that seems to her "emancipated," "modern," "the latest thing," and frowns upon "girls of principle," girls who are "blinkered" or "hunting for husbands with a lot of dough."

She "adores" writing essays for school whose subjects she copies out for her friend. Is Rabelais an enigma? Boileau said, "Love reason," and Alfred de Musset, "Love beyond reason!" etc.

Her letters revolve around school life and her readings (Sagan, Camus, *The Rebel*—described as "grueling"), the future, and existence in general. Her tone is vibrant, exalted. The proclamation "Life is worth living" frequently recurs. She writes of the ball she attended during the Yvetot carnival: "In a kind of unbridled whirl, I felt an incredible happiness I'd never felt before and was thinking out loud because I said 'I'm happy.'"

Not a word about her parents.

Undoubtedly these letters, while they seem to me sincere, are pervaded by a desire to demonstrate to Marie-Claude a kinship of tastes, sensations, and attitudes toward others and life in general. With her whimsical nature, disdain for authority, and reading of contemporary novels borrowed from the library of her engineer father, Marie-Claude is an enviable role model, who initiates the girl into a more sophisticated world.

The fragments of my inner discourse are better preserved, I sense, in the poems and quotes I copied into a red hardcover diary from 1958, a gift from a cheese supplier, which I've managed to hang on to through each of my moves. That is where the girl of '58 speaks her truth by proxy, in words that draw a romanticized portrait of her being, lift her out of what she considers the flatness and brutality of the language of her milieu.

Next to some twenty poems by Jacques Prévert are a handful by Jules Laforgue, Musset, and a few isolated verses:

I received life as a slap
And as one whistles at an unknown woman

I followed life without knowing anything about it.
        (Pierre Loizeau)

There are passages from Proust, all about memory, copied from *L'histoire de la littérature française* by Paul Crouzet. There are others whose exact origins I have forgotten:
        There is no real happiness except that of which
        we are aware while experiencing it. (Alexandre
        Dumas, fils)
        Each one of my desires has enriched me more
        than the always-deceitful possession of the object
        of my desire. (André Gide)

There you have the girl who is about to enter the summer camp.

She is real outside of me, her name recorded in black and white in the annals of the open-air sanatorium of S (that is, if they have not been discarded). Annie Duchesne. My maiden name, including my father's surname with its trumpeting cadence (so it seemed to me), a name I disliked, perhaps because it hailed from *the wrong side of the family*, according to my mother. I preferred hers, Duménil, softer, more muted. Duchesne, a name I lost six years later without regret, and perhaps with a certain relief, at the Rouen town hall, simultaneously endorsing my transfer to the bourgeoisie and the obliteration of S.

The place, too, is real. In my memory it has gradually

metamorphosed into a kind of castle, a cross between Les Sablonnières in *Le Grand Meaulnes* and the palace in *Last Year at Marienbad*. I tried to find it again in the autumn of 1995 while driving home from Saint-Malo, without success. I was forced to park in the Main Street of S and ask a tobacconist how to get to the sanatorium, and when she gazed back at me blankly, as if she had never heard of it, I added, "the old medico-educational institute, I believe." I only discovered today on the Internet that the place was once an abbey, founded in the Middle Ages. Demolished, rebuilt, and transformed over the centuries. Cannot be visited except on national heritage days.

In current photos, there remains no trace of its former vocation as an open-air sanatorium, transformed during the summer months into a large "health camp," able to accommodate two successive contingents of several hundred sickly or "temperamental" children, supervised by some thirty counselors, two gym teachers, a doctor, and a handful of nurses. Conversely, there is no mention at all of the site's historical interest on the postcard sent in late August 1958 to Odile—the other close friend from the convent school, but close in a different way from Marie-Claude because Odile is of peasant stock and the social affinities with the grocer's girl run deep, do not need to be spoken. When the two are together, it is enough to exchange a few words in dialect, laughing. On this postcard, which Odile photocopied for me several years ago, I see an aerial view of a stately and austere-looking group of old stone buildings with a faint ochre hue. Three wings of different heights and lengths form the shape of a T, whose perpendicular bar is slightly off center toward the right. The shortest wing makes one think of a chapel. The entrance is a monumental portico flanked by two porter's lodges. The assemblage of buildings seems to date from separate periods, though most of it is from the eighteenth century. A playing field is enclosed between two wings of the building. To the left of the portico are small postwar buildings. To the right is a park whose outer edges cannot be seen. The entire visible area in the photo is girded by a wall. On the back of the postcard is written *Aérium à S* [. . .]—Orne.

Just as I am about to send Annie Duchesne under the portico and through the door on that day of August 14, 1958, I am overwhelmed by apathy, often a sign that I am about to abandon my writing in the face of difficulties I cannot clearly define. It has nothing to do with a shortage of memories. In fact, I must hold myself back to keep the images from linking up with each other—an image of a room with an image of a dress and a tube of red Émail Diamant toothpaste (memory is a lunatic props-mistress), reducing me to the state of a spellbound viewer of a film utterly devoid of meaning. On the contrary, the problem I am up against is how to grasp the behavior of this girl, Annie D, and how to understand her happiness and suffering in relation to the rules and beliefs of French society half a century ago, to the norms everyone took for granted except for a small and marginal group from "progressive" society, to which neither she nor anyone else at the camp belonged.

The others.

I typed their first and last names into the Internet phone directory, starting with the boys. For the very common surnames, there were so many occurrences of people with the same given name I might as well not have searched at all. No clue as to which of the Jacques R's was the boy at the camp in the summer of 1958. Their identities dissolved in the crowd. Certain names I traced to homes in Lower Normandy left me convinced, perhaps wrongly, that they belonged to some of the people I was searching for, whom I recalled as living there, even in 1958, which would mean they had never migrated from their territory of youth. The idea disturbed me, as if by having moored themselves to a single spot, these people had remained the same, their unaltered geographical identity guaranteeing them a permanence of being.

I tried the girls' names, none of which seemed to me reliable. The women had undoubtedly taken their husbands' names, as I had done, and not responded to the directory's helpful invitation: "List your maiden name so your friends from before can find you!"

I expanded my search on Google. On Copains d'avant, I identified, with absolute certainty, Didier D, a former student at the Maisons-Alfort veterinary school, and, then, albeit with less conviction, Guy A, a native of the North, who appeared on several sports sites in Lille and the surrounding area.

I returned to the phone directory and reentered the names. I sat riveted to the screen, perched at the edge of a sort of limbo from whose glittering depths I attempted to extract, one by one, beings it had engulfed and kept inside itself since the summer of '58.

Were these the same people, whose precise whereabouts France Télécom circled in blue on the map? Were they really there, underneath the dark smear of a roof revealed by an aerial photo, enlarged to the maximum degree and circled like a bull's-eye by the same blue geolocation loop?

I toyed with the idea of calling these people, even those I wasn't sure about, under the pretext of conducting a survey on the holiday camps of the fifties and sixties. I could pose as a journalist and ask questions such as, Were you at S in the summer of 1958? Do you remember the counselors, like H, the head counselor? And a girl counselor—well, actually not for long, she was transferred to the medical secretary's office, her name was Annie Duchesne? Quite tall, with long brown hair and glasses. What could you tell me about her? They would probably ask why I wanted to know. Or say I had dialed the wrong number. Or hang up on me.

Later I wondered why I'd wanted to do that, what exactly I'd been after. It wasn't to confirm that no one remembered

Annie D in the slightest, even less to discover that they did (a terrifying prospect). I wanted only one thing, to hear their voices, though the chances that I would recognize them were slim. I wanted physical, tangible proof of their existence, as if to continue writing I needed them to be alive, as if I needed to be writing about what is alive, to be endangered in the way one is when writing about the living and not in the state of tranquility that prevails when people die and are consigned to the immateriality of fictional characters. There is a need to make writing an untenable enterprise, to atone for its power (not its ease, no one feels less ease in writing than me) out of an imaginary terror of consequences.

Unless, now that I think of it, there is some perverse desire in me to make sure they're still alive in order to compromise them, as I attend to my business of disclosure: to be their final Judgment.

This time she entered. Naturally, everything she had imagined over the previous weeks about the open-air sanatorium of S is immediately erased by the sight of the monumental stone staircase, the long pillared refectory, the huge dormitories with dizzyingly high ceilings, the dark narrow hallway on the top floor of the building, with door after door of counselors' rooms. In her room at the very end of the hall, her roommate Jeannie, with thick curly brown hair and big black-rimmed glasses, has laid claim to the bed by the window, arranged her belongings in one half of the closet. The exuberant self-assurance the girl displayed earlier, in front of the train station, has vanished. As she meets the other girls as they arrive, she finds they all conduct themselves with ease and determination. Nothing appears to surprise them.

For her, everything is new.

On the first night, she lies awake, unsettled by the breathing of her roommate, who fell asleep the moment her head hit the pillow. She has never slept in the same room as someone she does not know. She feels the space belongs to her roommate more than it does to her.

The other counselors come from lycées and teachers colleges. Many already teach. A few work as educators all year long at the sanatorium. She is the only one who attends a religious institution. Much as she loathes the Saint-Michel convent school, she has no experience of a secular world in which, for example, the fifteenth of August is simply the day the children arrive at camp, and not the Feast of the Assumption of Mary into Heaven. For the first time in her life she will not go to Mass for Assumption. On the first day at lunch, she's asked what *bahut* she goes to, and she answers, after a moment's hesitation—for her, a *bahut* is a steamer trunk, or slang for a taxi—"Lycée Jeanne-d'Arc in Rouen." Then they want to know if she knows such-and-such a girl, and she has to admit that she has only just enrolled for the fall, and that until now she has attended a religious school.

She is disconcerted by the mingling of the sexes, unprepared for simple camaraderie between boys and girls employed to do the same job. The situation is unfamiliar. Basically, she only knows how to talk to boys with the kind of verbal sparring, at once enticing and derisive, that girls use when a group of boys follows them in the streets—defending themselves while leading them on. At the meeting held before the children's arrival, she glances around at the fifteen-odd boys and finds that none correspond to her dream of falling passionately in love.

Two images from the first days:

On the sunny lawn at lunchtime, in front of the doors to the refectory, a group of almost one hundred children, conducted by the elegant director in a jacket and trousers the color of autumn leaves, sing softly at first and then with increasing volume until the sound is a thundering roar that sends shivers down the spine. The volume inches down again to a barely audible murmur as the children sing: *Papa! Maman! This child has only one eye! Papa! Maman! This child has only one tooth! Brother, what a bother, a kid with only one eye! Gracious, what a nuisance, a kid with only one tooth!*

On the grass in the park, twelve teenage girls in uniform (blue jumpers and shorts) dance with their arms solidly linked, exuberantly led by a blond ponytailed counselor, positioned in the middle, who makes them kick out and step to the right, then to the left, singing *I have holes in my shoes, I have holes in my shoes / I'm a zazou, I'm a zazou**

I perceive in the persistence of these memories, the girl's fascination with a rigorously organized world, ruled by blasts from a pea whistle and the rhythm of marching songs, all in an atmosphere of gaiety and freedom, a society in which everyone is in a happy mood, from the director to the nurses, and for the first time the girl finds adults bearable. It is a kind of closed, ideal world where all needs—food, games, and activities—are met with abundance, a largesse that nothing about life at the convent school in Yvetot would have allowed her to believe possible.

I perceive a desire to acclimatize to the new environment but also a pervasive fear of being unable to do so, of never reaching the heights of the blond counselor, the ideal. She does not know any songs free of references to God. Great is her relief upon learning, on the second day, that she will not be in charge of a single group of children but act as a "floating" counselor, who replaces the others on their days off.

---

* A member of a French youth subculture of the World War II period, associated with swing, jazz and bebop, and loud, oversized clothing such as zootsuits. The term was used for the first time in France in 1938 in the Johnny Hess song 'Je suis swing': *je suis swing, je suis swing, zazou, zazou, zazou zazou dé.*

She has been at the camp for three days. It is Saturday evening. The children have all been put to bed in the dorms. I see her, as I will dozens of times thereafter, clattering down the stairs, flight after flight with her roommate, wearing jeans, a sleeveless sailor top, and white sandals with straps. She has removed her glasses and unpinned her hair so it hangs long and loose down her back. She is very excited, it is her first real party.

I don't know whether music was already playing when they arrived in the cellar, away from the central building, under the infirmary or some other locale, or whether he was already there among the people crowding around the phonograph and choosing records. What is certain is that he was the first to ask her to dance. It's a rock 'n' roll number. She is embarrassed about dancing so badly (it is possible she told him so, by way of an apology). Guided by his grip on her hand, she twirls around with lunging strides, and her sandals make a clacking sound on the cement floor. She is unsettled by the way he stares at her as he spins her around. No one has ever looked at her with such a heavy gaze. "He" is H, the head instructor: tall, blond, burly, with a bit of a spare tire around the middle. She does not even ask herself if she likes him, or if she finds him attractive. He does not look much older than the other counselors, but to her he seems more a man than a boy, on account of his function. She sees him as on the side that rules, in the same way she views his female counterpart L, the head counselor for girls. Earlier, she had eaten lunch at the same table as him, daunted and very embarrassed at dessert because she didn't know how to eat her peach without making a mess. She did not for a moment imagine that she could interest him and is dumbfounded.

Still dancing, he backs up toward the wall, continuing to stare at her. The lights go off. He pulls her violently to his chest, crushes his mouth against hers. Protests ring out in the darkness. Someone presses the button to turn the lights on again. She understands that it was he who turned them off. She cannot look up at him, overcome by a heady panic. She cannot believe what is happening. He whispers, Shall we go outside? She says yes, they cannot carry on like this in front of the others. Then they are outside, walking along the walls of the sanatorium with their arms around each other. The night is cold. Near the refectory, facing the dark lawn, he presses her up against the wall and rubs himself against her. She feels his sex prod at her belly through her jeans. He is going too fast. She is not prepared for this kind of urgency, ardor. She does not feel anything. She is subjugated by his desire for her, a man's desire, wild, unbridled, nothing like the slow, cautious approach of the boy from the previous spring. She does not ask where they are going. When did it occur to her that he was taking her to a room? Or maybe he told her?

They are in her room, in the dark. She does not see what he is doing. Even then, she still believes they will continue to kiss and caress each other through their clothes, on the bed. He says: "Take your clothes off." From the moment he invited her to dance, she has done everything he has told her to do. There is no difference between what she does and what happens to her. She lies beside him naked on the narrow bed. She has no time to get used to this total nudity, his naked male body. Right away she feels the mass and rigidity of his member pushing between her thighs. He thrusts hard. It hurts her. She tells him she's a virgin, as a matter of self-defense or explanation. She cries out. He grumbles: "I'd rather you came than kick up such a fuss!" She would like to be anywhere but there, but she does not leave. She feels cold. She could get up, turn the lights back on, tell him to get dressed and leave. Or get dressed herself and leave him in the lurch, return to the party. She could have. But I know the idea never crossed her mind. For her there was no turning back, things had to run their course. She had no right to abandon this man in the state he was in, raging with desire, all because of her. It was unimaginable that he had not chosen, *elected* her over all the other girls.

The rest unfolds like an X-rated film in which the woman is completely out of sync with the man because she has no idea what will happen next. Only he knows. He is the master, always one step ahead. He has her slide down to his lower belly, her mouth on his cock. A thick jet of sperm explodes in her face, gushing all the way into her nostrils. Scarcely five minutes have passed since they entered the room.

In my memory I am unable to find a single emotion, let alone a thought. The girl on the bed watches things happen to her that she never would have imagined happening an hour before. That is all.

He turns on the light and asks which bar of soap belongs to her, the one to the right or the left of the sink. He lathers his sex, hers too. They sit down on the bed again. She offers him hazelnut milk chocolate from her parents' store. He jokes: Once you get paid, buy whiskey! But whiskey is a luxury spirit her parents do not sell. Anyway, alcohol disgusts her.

Her roommate will be back from the party at any moment. They put their clothes on. She follows him to his room, which as head counselor he is not obliged to share. She has surrendered all will, entirely absorbed by his, and by his experience as a man. (Never at any moment will she be in his thoughts. To this day, it remains a mystery to me.)

I do not know exactly when she inwardly consents to losing her virginity. It is not from resignation; she wants to lose it, collaborates. He tried to penetrate her countless times—I don't remember how many—and she sucked him instead because he never managed to get inside. He concedes, as if to excuse her: "I'm big."

He repeats that he wants her to come. She cannot: he handles her sex too roughly. She could perhaps if he caressed her sex with his mouth, but she does not ask him to do so. It's a shameful thing for a girl to ask. She only does what he wants.

Her submission is not to him but to an indisputable, universal law: that of a savagery in the male to which she would have had to be subjected, sooner or later. That this law is brutal and dirty is just the way things are.

He utters words she has never heard before, which remove her from the world of adolescent girls to that of men, from whispered obscenities and snickers to a realm of unadulterated sex:

I masturbated this afternoon.

So I guess they're all dykes at your school?

He wants to talk and so they quietly talk in each other's arms, facing the window whose wall is covered with children's coloring pages. He is from the Jura, a gym teacher at a technical college in Rouen, he has a fiancée. He is twenty-two. They reveal little things about themselves. She remarks that she has wide hips. He answers, "You have a woman's hips." She is happy. It has become a normal relationship. They must have slept for a while.

The sun has risen, she goes back to her room. The moment she leaves him, she is struck with disbelief at all that has happened. She remains in a stupor, as if intoxicated by the event, which needs to be articulated in order to be real. She says to her roommate, already washed and dressed to go down to breakfast, "I slept with the head counselor."

I do not know if it has occurred to her yet that it has been a "night of love," her first.

It is the first time I've gone back over that night of August 16–17, 1958, with a deep sense of satisfaction. I think I have come as close as possible to the reality of it, which was neither horror nor shame, only an obedience to what was happening, the lack of meaning in the things that happened. I can go no further in this sort of willed migration into my being at scarcely eighteen years of age, and its ignorance of what comes next, of the Sunday just begun.

At lunchtime in the refectory, amidst the racket, she sits at the end of a table supervising a dozen loudmouthed little boys. She cannot bring herself to swallow a single mouthful of the slimy, blackish vegetables on her plate (eggplant, which she has never eaten before). It seems to me her chest has been tight, her heart in her mouth, from the moment she entered the cellar the previous evening. Suddenly he appears between the refectory columns and moves between the tables, inspecting. He stops at hers. From the opposite end of the table, between two parallel rows of little boys, he stares at her in silence. She has not seen him since the night before. She sees that gaze—she has her glasses on—descending on her, pinning her down, pressing her to remember what she did the night before. She lowers her eyes. She cannot stand this obtrusive stare: she is a child among others, guilty of misconduct. (Much later, I will berate myself for not having returned that gaze, fraught with the memory of the previous night and a sense of collusion he must have expected in return, but which the girl of that morning is unable to interpret.)

I can only write about what happens next by jumping from one image or scene to another, scenes that in reality would usually not have lasted more than several minutes, even seconds, but which memory has distended out of all proportion, as if it had added a little extra to each passage. In this sense I am like the person who is up against the wall in a game of Red Light, Green Light, and turns around to see the players' frozen poses but cannot see the movements that preceded them. The progression of life between two images has long been invisible to me.

I see her in the afternoon reading the first pages of *The Human Condition* in a pocket edition. With each page she reads she forgets the one before. After the murder of the sleeping man beneath the mosquito net, she loses track of the story. She has never experienced this inability to read.

I see her on Sunday night in H's room, after the children are in bed and the counselors are free, except for those who supervise the dorms in the bluish glow of the night-lights. Did he arrange the meeting when they saw each other by chance in the afternoon, or has she come to him of her own accord? In any case, she cannot imagine that they will not spend the night together after what happened the night before. He is lying on the bed, she sitting next to him, close to the edge. He toys with the flowered scarf she has slipped into the neckline of the blue cardigan she wears against her bare skin. She commits the first offense. As innocently as she had offered him chocolate the night before, with the same ignorance about boys and no conception of the wound she is inflicting on his pride (which, over the years, I have come to find increasingly difficult to believe), she says, referring to a blond-bearded counselor with a rugby man's build: "After the Beard, you're the best-looking guy in the camp."

She thinks she is paying him a compliment and does not in the least seize the irony of his quick retort, "Golly, thanks," because she adds:

"But it's true!"

She says this with no intent to hurt, states it as a truth that exists outside the two of them and can in no way signify that she prefers the Beard.

His face darkens and she sees her blunder, but just as soon dismisses it. She has slipped into the autism of her desire for another night with H, convinced she will have it because of what happened between them the night before—what they did and what they have not done yet. He is her lover. She waits for a sign. She may be disconcerted when no sign comes.

In the following scene, he has left the room. She remains standing, waiting, and believing he will return.

It is not he who enters the room next but Claude L, a boy from Brittany with curly brown hair. He makes it plain that there is no point in her staying, that H will not be back. I think she asks if H went to see the blond teacher, Catherine P. Claude L does not answer. Maybe he laughs.

(From this moment on, I am incapable of entering the mind of the girl of S, I can only describe her gestures and actions, and record the words that are spoken: others' and, less often, her own.)

I see her in the harsh light of H's room, dazed, incredulous, maybe in tears, diving into a corner to hide between the wall and door when someone knocks. She flattens herself against the wall behind the door, which stands wide open, and hears Monique C laugh and say to the curly-haired guy (who, she realizes with horror, has silently signaled her presence), "What's she doing there, is she drunk?" The girl comes out from behind the door and shows herself, stands before them shoeless, three feet away, and Monique looks her up and down, amused. I no longer know what the girl said in the way of an entreaty, the words she used that shame has buried since (perhaps

something to do with whether H was with the blonde), nor what contemptuous reply she must have received for her to then beseech Monique, "But aren't we friends?" and for Monique C to retort with violence, a kind of revulsion: "I don't know you from a hole in the wall! Who do you think you are?"

Again and again, I go over the scene, whose horror remains acute: that of having been so miserable, like a dog who begs to be petted and receives a kick instead. But I never break through the obscurity of a present gone for fifty years now. My viewing and reviewing of the scene leaves intact and incomprehensible another girl's loathing for me.

All that is certain is that Annie D, her parents' spoiled little girl, the brilliant pupil, is at this precise moment an object of contempt and derision in the eyes of Monique C and Claude L, and all those she would have longed to have as peers.

She is no longer in H's room. At what point on that Sunday evening, lost, distraught, did she stumble into— or willingly join—the little band of counselors, both girls and boys, united by a twilight hankering to celebrate, raise Cain, and also, perhaps, by a vague desire to rag the new arrivals on these first days of camp? Whatever the case, I see her in the corridor, howling in protest, blinded by her hair that is soaked with water from a bucket emptied on top of her, no doubt amidst a chorus of *Hooyah, hooyah!* or some other battle cry, since become a ritual in hazings. They hoot with laughter: "You look just like Juliette Gréco!" Through her wet hair, she sees H standing at the door to his room, motionless, massive. He smiles with the indulgence of the older, responsible person observing the antics of lycée kids. (Today, it would be easy for me to assume that the group, already in the know, had plotted to lead me to H's room *just for fun.*) She commits her second blunder of the evening. She breaks away from the group, calls his name and, laughing, cries for help. She tells him what the others said, that she looks like Juliette Gréco. It seems natural to appeal to him for rescue because of the night before, their nakedness. She is about to throw herself into his arms, but his arms remain hanging by his sides. He continues to smile, without saying a word. He turns and goes back to his room (no doubt increasingly convinced that the girl is an idiot, and he is not about to be saddled with an imbecile who takes herself for Juliette Gréco).

On this gray November Sunday in 2014, I watch the girl who was me watch him turn his back on her in front of all the others, the first man with whom she has ever been naked, who took pleasure in her body all night long. There is not a thought in her head, nothing inside but the memory of their two bodies, their gestures, and what was accomplished—whether she wanted it or not. She is seized by the panic of loss and a sense of abandonment that cannot be justified.

She is lost—a rag-doll girl. She doesn't care what happens to her and lets herself be led by the excited little group with the docility of a totally insensible being. They are in a new building to the left of the abbey, a huge room with greenish walls and a naked bulb suspended from the ceiling. She does not have her glasses on. They continue to insist that it is the room shared by the director's two secretaries, away for the weekend. She is surprised at how they make themselves at home, putting on records by Robert Lamoureux and Fernand Raynaud, producing glasses and white wine. She does not realize (and will only learn the following day) that it is all a prank at her expense. In fact, the room belongs to the two phys ed instructors, Guy A and Jacques R, who is draping himself around her on the bed where a group of them are sitting. Had they already begun to "take the piss out of her," as she was told a few days later by Claudine D, the counselor with a port-wine stain across one cheek, having learned of the night she had spent with the head instructor and witnessed her disgrace in the corridor?

She hears them laugh and tell dirty stories, absent and numb. (Just now, the final scene of Barbara Loden's *Wanda* glides across the moment I am writing about: Wanda in a nightclub, between two revelers. Mute, she takes the cigarette one gives her, turning her head right, then left. She is no longer present. "I'm worthless," she'd said, a moment before. Freeze-frame on her face, which little by little *dissolves*.)

Fifteen years before the making of *Wanda*, its sequel was shot in a room in S. They've extinguished the light bulb and lie in couples on the beds and on the floor. Records continue to play on the phonograph. She lies on the floor on a mattress, in a sleeping bag with Jacques R. Both are naked from the waist down. He kisses her over and over. She does not like his flaccid lips. He pushes his sex toward hers. It is not as thick as H's. She says no and that she is a virgin. He leaves a wet spot between her thighs. It seems to me she weeps, listening in the dark to the other boys, who jokingly report upon the progress of their operations with the girls, while Dalida sings, *Je pars avec la joie au cœur lalalalayéyéyéyé / Je pars vers le bonheur.*

He tries again to enter her. He thrashes around, without brutality, in the stubborn determination of his desire. She's afraid he'll succeed. She does not think to get up and leave. The situation is neither good nor bad, but somewhere between distress and the consolation a substitute body provides: the same male desire in a different body. Her body is only on loan; she is fiercely determined to prevent it from being entered. Undoubtedly she is already possessed by the desire to "give herself"—the expression in use at the time—only to H, the man who had begged her to do just that, the night before, and has now rejected her.

I have followed the girl, image by image, since the evening she and her roommate entered the cellar and H invited the girl to dance, but it is impossible to grasp the logical sequence, the gradual shifts that have brought her to the state she is in now.

All I can say is that on Monday, August 18, at dawn, when she returns to her room, where, again, her roommate is already up and dressed, she considers what happened with Jacques R in the sleeping bag as completely insignificant, null and void. (That is, after panicking when she removed her jeans and saw that she was bleeding, then realized with relief that her period had arrived eight days early.)

I see Annie D, whose desire has reached its peak. Certainly, she cannot rise any higher in her denial of everything that is not her desire for H. She believes he will still want her, and continues to believe it even when, on the night after the "hazing," she goes to his room and meets with indignant, scathing rejection on the grounds that she has "gone with [Jacques] R." She continues to believe it after learning that the blond schoolmistress Catherine, engaged to a conscript in Algeria, as attested by her ring with a blue stone and the letters stamped *FM* set down next to her plate each day, has taken her place in the head counselor's bed.

She wants him to make all the moves, perform all the gestures that signal his desire for her. She wants him to consume himself with pleasure in her body. She expects none for herself.

She does not give up but simply waits for him to want her, one night, on a whim, out of boredom with the blonde, or out of pity—the reason hardly matters. Her need to give him mastery of her body makes her a stranger to any sense of dignity.

Because of his heavy-lidded eyes, pouting lips, and massive frame, she thinks he looks like Marlon Brando. She does not care that other female counselors murmur to each other that he's all brawn, no brains. Her private name for him is "the Archangel."

One day during an hour off, she enters the cathedral of S, careful not to be seen by any of the counselors, who would taunt her with glee, especially not the schoolteacher from Provence who sings her a ribald song to the tune of "Ave Maria" while looking at her ironically. The God she beseeches is only a stand-in for H, the true god, who has forsaken her, indifferent to her misery and despair, and chosen the blonde instead. Oh Lord, only say the word and my soul will be healed.

As I write it occurs to me, as it never has before, that the blonde may have wanted to seize a position I had occupied by chance, and which, betrothed or not, she could not have borne to relinquish to a great bumbling beanpole with Coke-bottle glasses, which is undoubtedly how she'd seen me from the first day of camp, when we had our X-rays done one after the other at the infirmary. Others were probably of the same opinion. I never heard them criticize the blonde's two-timing of her fiancé. Unconsciously they acquiesced to the transient pairing of the burly head instructor and the perky schoolmistress whose figure, unveiled one day in a swimsuit, would raise wolf whistles from the boys, along with their usual pun based on the expression "pinup," the index finger standing to attention in a facsimile of an erection. I must have agreed. I thought her more beautiful, more everything than me. In 2003, I tersely summarized: "She is, I am not."

As I advance, the former simplicity of the story deposited in memory disappears. To go all the way to the end of '58 means agreeing to the demolition of all the interpretations I've assembled over the years. No glossing over. I am not constructing a fictional character but deconstructing the girl I was.

A suspicion: obscurely, I may have wished to unfold this period of my life to test the limits of writing, push the closeness to reality as far as it would go (and I would go so far as to judge my previous books as vague approximations in this regard). I might also challenge the figure of the writer that others see and mirror back to me, savage it, ruthlessly denounce an imposture that goes to the tune of "I'm not who you think I am," which, as it happens, closely echoes a pun the male counselors will start to taunt me with in the following days: "Je ne suis pucelle que vous croyez, I'm no longer the virgin you think I am!"

Now for the next part, the writing of what comes next, when H has ceased to want her and she does not want Jacques R.

How do we enter the girl's enraptured drifting, her sense of living the most exalted days of her existence, which makes her impervious to all the mockery and sarcasm, the insulting remarks.

In what mode—tragic, lyrical, romantic (even comic would not be difficult)—is one to relate the girl's experience in S, the tranquility and hubris which was judged by others—all the others—as insanity and whoredom?

Should I write that, ten years before the May revolution, I was sublimely bold, a pioneer of sexual freedom, avatar of Bardot in *And God Created Woman*, which I had not yet seen, and adopt the jubilant tone of the letter I have before me, written to Marie-Claude in late August '58? "As for me, all is for the best in the best of all possible worlds. [. . .] I spent the night with [. . .] the head counselor. Does this shock you? I also slept with one of the phys ed teachers the following day. So there you have it: I'm amoral and cynical. The worst of it is that I feel no remorse. It is actually so simple that two minutes later, it's slipped my mind." Should I judge the girl of S according to the mores of today, when nothing sexual, apart from incest and rape, is reprehensible, and on the Internet I can read headings like "Vanessa will spend her holidays at a swingers' hotel"? Or should I adopt the view of French society in 1958, which reduced a girl's entire worth to a question of "conduct," and say that in her naïveté and lack of guile she is pathetic, laying the entire blame at her feet? Must I, as of now, move back and forth between one historical vision and another, between 1958 and 2014? I dream of a sentence that would contain them both, seamlessly, by way of a new syntax.

Every night is a revel. She is there at every *sur-pat*, listening to records in someone's darkened room. She is game for all the dares and double dares, pushing the director's Citroën 2CV into the refectory, or scaling the walls for a nocturnal tear around the deserted streets of S. She does not want to miss a single moment of the present, or the promise of each evening. I see her:

perched on a barstool, Chez Graindorge, drinking gin in defiance of her deep distaste for alcohol, which has to do with the drunkards at her parents' café

walking "tightrope" on top of the abbey wall, afraid of falling because she's three sheets to the wind

trudging arm in arm between two boys, in the middle of a gang, howling the words of *De profundis morpionibus*, ballad of the pubic lice, feeling exalted and superior as one does when walking in a city where everyone's asleep

sitting with her head on a shoulder—whose?— in a cinema, watching *Kanał*, a film from a Soviet bloc country; the images and subtitles are nothing but a blur because she's not wearing her glasses.

most of all, racing down the two flights of stairs with a Gauloise between her fingers, to join the group that varies according to staff rotation in the dorms, or the formation of couples who prefer the privacy of a room—eager to leap into the euphoria of the group.

I know that her happiness is real and have no doubt at all that she is conscious of its reality, with the kind of consciousness whose necessity is evoked in the quotation she has transcribed into the red appointment diary: There is no real happiness except that of which we are aware while experiencing it. (Alexandre Dumas, fils)

Inside her, there is nothing left of Yvetot, the boarding school, the nuns, or the café-grocery. In the middle of September, her parents will come to visit with her uncle and aunt. When she sees them emerge from the 4CV at the door of the sanatorium, with their big sweeping gestures and honking voices, she will feel nothing but the astonishment of having forgotten them so thoroughly in a month. With a vague sense of pity she will find they look old.

She is dazzled by her freedom, its dizzying expanse. She is earning money for the first time and buys whatever strikes her fancy, pastries, red Émail Diamant toothpaste. There is nothing she wants more than to live this way, always—to dance, laugh, horse about, sing lewd songs, flirt.

She floats in the lightness of being cut loose from her mother's watchful gaze.

(The constancy of this happiness is belied by a less glorious image: that of a girl alone in the night, faintly staggering toward the toilets near the refectory, down a corridor flanked by a long row of columns, in a mind reduced to a sort of puddle that drifts above a body that eludes her, yet with the acuity that white wine leaves in its wake, asking herself *what she has become*.)

Since H, she has needed to feel a man's body pressed against hers, feel his hands, an erect penis. The consolatory erection.

She is proud to be the object of lust, and quantity seems to her the gauge of her seduction value. She feels a kind of collector's pride (exemplified by the following memory: one day in a meadow, after kissing a chemistry student in S on holiday, I boast about the number of boys from camp whom I have been with, one way or another). They waste no time on niceties, there is no deferral of her desire for their desire. They get right to it, and believe her reputation entitles them to do so. While kissing her, they lift her skirt or tug at the zip of her jeans. Three minutes, between the thighs, always. She says that she's a virgin, doesn't want them inside. She never has an orgasm.

She goes from one to the other and never becomes attached, not even to Pierre D, with whom she spent several nights in the big dorm for boys, which he supervised through a window in a small adjoining room, who said "I love you"— he was the first boy ever to do so—and she replied:

"No, it's just desire."

"I assure you, Annie, it's true."

"No."

Here, I have a sense of glorifying the self of 1958, which I cannot say is dead, because it completely overwhelmed me when I watched *Love Is My Profession* again, with Brigitte Bardot, on February 8, 1999, and immediately wrote in my journal: "Stunned to see how much like Bardot I was in my behavior with men in '58, my blunders, my spontaneity, telling one that I had flirted with the other. No rules whatsoever. It's the image of myself that I've repressed the most." I feel I am vindicating that dauntless self, though later I was dogged by the idea that it would take control of my life and drive me to ruin, not that I was able to say exactly what that meant.

But what I discover through my immersion in that summer is an immense desire, impossible to put into words, which reduces to insignificance the cheerful willingness of girls who, with full awareness, do everything, fellatio, etc., the S/M rites with built-in safety measures, the uninhibited sexuality of all those who do not know *the despair of the flesh*.

Their names and surnames—eight including H and Jacques R—are listed one below the other in the last pages of a little diary from 1963, which I used to write *Happening*. I can no longer say why I made that inventory, which appears more than four years after my time at S.

Undoubtedly I had already listed them in my appointment diary for 1958, which my mother burned at the end of the sixties, along with my journal from the time, certain that it was all to the good, for the sake of my social salvation, todestroy the evidence of the bad life her daughter had led before she went onto be a teacher of literature, marry "well," and bear two children. Her daughter: her pride, her rage and crowning achievement. The truth survived the fire.

A historical snare to which the writing of the self is prone: though for many years it served as material evidence of my "misconduct" (an expression which has itself become "historical," dated), and though it is not short, this list by no means shocks me now, in 2015. To attune the sensibility of readers today to the disgrace heaped upon the girl of S, for the purpose of comparison, I will have to present another list that includes the coarse taunts, the hooting and jeering, the insults passed off as jokes, whereby the male counselors made her an object of scorn and derision, they whose verbal hegemony went unquestioned and was even admired by the female counselors; they who evaluated the erotic potential of all the girls, classified as "tight-assed" or "goody-goodies" versus "up for it" or "good rides." In other words, enumerate the jubilant name-calling "all in jest," the jokes called after her to amuse the gallery of both genders, especially those belonging to the First Sex, always ready to go one better than their peers at her expense, while the Second Sex looks on smiling, never disapproving:

I'm not the virgin you think I am
You've read too many novels
Did you buy your sunglasses (which I think are pretty) at the five-and-ten?
You have an ass like a washbowl
Psst, there goes the medical body (my pedagogical failings having quickly been detected, I was sent to replace the infirmary secretary, who was on vacation)

The phrases with double meanings, combined with the gesture of touching the testicles:
Seek and you shall find
I'm not plugged in

The travestied songs, intoned as she walks by:
Si t'en veux plus, je la remets dans ma culotte
Cha-cha-cha des thons, etc.[*]

That is not to forget their favorite proverb: *Man proposes, woman disposes . . .* But this one disposes badly.

And finally, the word that authorized the outpouring of obscenities, along with the raucous denial of her intellectual abilities, *You with the math–Latin baccalauréat, ha ha, I'd have let you leave school at fourteen*, the offending word only marginally softened by a turn of phrase that was

---

[*] "If you've had enough, I'll put it back in my pants, Cha cha cha, do the tuna dance!

common currency in the summer of '58: "A whore around the edges."

It was written, with my toothpaste, in big red letters, free of understatement, on the mirror over the sink in my room: *Long live whores.* (The phrasing incurred the wrath of my roommate—a good girl, who only had one fling over that summer—and elicited from me the following query, "Is it the plural that bothers you?")

The girl of '58 does not take offense. She even looks amused, accustomed to this mocking aggressiveness with herself as its object. Perhaps she sees it as further proof of the error of their judgment. There's been a mistake. She is not what they say she is.

To what may we attribute that certainty today? To her virginity, which she resolutely preserves, her brilliant academic record, her reading of Sartre? It can be explained, above all, by her mad love for H, the Archangel—as she persists in calling him, going so far as to do so in front of Claudine D, who taps the side of her head and tells her she's *totally deranged*—and by the way she has absorbed him within herself, through incorporation, which holds her above shame.

It was not shame (of this I am certain) that fixed the memory of the words in red toothpaste. It was the falsity of the insult, of their judgment, of the lack of coherence between "whore" and her. I see nothing from that period that could be described as shame.

Not even when, at lunchtime, her attention is drawn by the sound of laughter as five or six male counselors jostle and elbow each other in front of the bulletin board next to the dining room. She moves toward them and sees a crumpled sheet of paper pinned to the board with thumbtacks, next to the announcements, for everyone to see: a confiding letter written the previous night to her great friend Odile, which she tore up and threw in the wastepaper basket before starting another. The boys gather around, hooting with laughter and quoting lines from her letter, "So it makes you crazy when H puts his hand on your shoulder as he walks by?" She calls them bastards, cries that they have no right, asks which of them had the nerve. They tell her it was the line cook, who found the letter in the trash, and pinned it up a few minutes earlier. She tears it off the board. She wants to see the cook. He needs no encouragement, emerges from the kitchen grinning from ear to ear, delighted that his initiative has put them all in stitches.

I see him now, V, in his forties, blond and baby-faced in a blue-and-white-checked jacket, kind and friendly like his wife, who is also a cook. His self-satisfaction, his braggardly air. Did I want to slap him? He is unslappable, backed by all the others, who meanwhile have dissolved into a wall of laughter all around her. Oh, come now, they say, where's the harm? Does she realize that her allusion to the law, reiterated with rage ("You had no right"), will not affect them in the least? That the fault lies entirely with her for writing such a sentimental letter and leaving it out in the open? That no one needs to use kid gloves with a whore around the edges, moronically in love with a guy who spends his nights with a blonde who is much more of a stunner than she, and that she has no defense against the image they have of her? It is that image which gives the cook the right to display her letter and everyone else the right to laugh. I do not recall her perceiving a link between what they think of her and what they do to her. What may concern her more than anything is the likelihood that H has read the letter and does not give a damn about her, probably cares even less than the others.

Today I see a similarity between the scene of the letter and the night with H. Common to both was my complete inability to convince, to fully assert my point of view. When I go back over the corridor scene, little by little, the girl in the middle becomes depersonalized, is no longer me or even Annie D. What happened in the corridor at the camp takes us back to time immemorial, all over the planet. Everywhere on earth, with every day that dawns, a woman stands surrounded by men ready to *throw stones at her*.

About the scene of the girl of '58 in the middle of the circle: today, when I strip away the stigma it took on in my mind after I began to study philosophy the following October and which kept me from talking about what happened until just last summer, when I told a woman novelist friend, I know that the girl of '58 is not ashamed of what she wrote in her letter to Odile. She is in a stupor. It is beyond her comprehension that the opprobrium should fall on her and not the cook; she cannot believe that these repugnant actions are applauded, that no one comes to her defense. The line they have overstepped proves beyond a doubt that they do not see her as they do the other female counselors, and that with her they may do as they please. She is not their equal. She does not have the same worth. They don't know her from a hole in the wall, and who does she think she is, in the words of Monique C. The ease—the lightness—of her position in the group has been compromised.

But not her need to be part of it.

I do not even think it occurred to her that for the sake of dignity and self-preservation, she should feel obliged to withdraw from the group and go to bed early, as some of the female counselors did. She cannot be deprived of all the things that since her arrival at the camp have proved an amazing discovery—the rapture of living with other young people in a place removed from the rest of society, under the distant and benevolent rule of a small group of adults; the exaltation of belonging to a community soldered by short-sheeted beds, obscene puns and songs, a fraternity based on derision and vulgarity; a euphoria of the entire being, as if one's own youth were multiplied by that of the others in a sort of collective intoxication.

This happiness—in my memory—was redoubled by the presence of hundreds of children whose games, laughter, and shouting blurred together into a kind of dull roar that filled the space from the morning on, thundering at mealtime in the huge refectory, tapering off in the evening, under the high ceilings of dorms bathed in the blue glow of night-lights.

Because the joy of the group is more powerful than humiliation, she wants to remain with the others. I see her want to be like them so badly that she resorts to imitation. She copies their verbal tics and expressions: "Don't tell us the story of your life, it's full of holes," "In the words of the potato masher, shut up and press on," "When pigs fly!" "If you lie, Granny will die," even if in the long run she finds it painfully tedious. Or, like them, she punctuates her sentences with a drawling "*euh là . . .*" specific to Lower Normandy. Within the group, the students and former alumni of the École normale for schoolteachers in Rouen form a cheerful, anticlerical tribe, united by the certainty of belonging to an elite. The girl envies their solidarity, the proud group they make, both boys and girls. She listens to them talk about themselves and "la Norm," as they refer to their school. She does not utter a word about her Catholic boarding school, knowing she is disqualified from the start, on account of "her" nuns ("every last one of them sexually repressed"), the obligatory prayers, her religious education that it titillates the others to ridicule.

The reversibility of humiliation: Since rumor has it that a newly arrived counselor, André R, boasted of "having it off" with a girl of fourteen at his previous camp, the group decides to teach him a lesson. (Though given the group's usual laddish criteria, it might have been expected to judge the boy "inept" and leave it that.) The girl of '58 thinks the lesson is an excellent idea. First, he needs to be plied with drink—she'll take care of it. I see her dancing with him, repeatedly passing him the bottle of white wine, from which she drinks only a drop. Later, I see him blindfolded, stripped to the waist, and standing on a chair, while with great application and a brush dipped in bright red paint, the Beard carefully traces a huge phallus on his back, with drops of sperm at the tip. I hear them laugh: "There, we've made you a nice big *zob*!" André R puts up no resistance. One is hard pressed to get free of the game if one is alone.

This time she is in the players' circle.

Each morning as I am about to start writing, a kind of tableau appears before me—a castle and its grounds, completely overrun by the vague forms of children, dressed in blue from head to toe, and:

Them—the counselors, an obscene choir of voices, chiefly male, their laughter and their songs

Him—H, far in the distance, at once one of *them* and hovering above: the Angel of the painting

Her—Annie D, stage center in all of the scenes with them.

There is no self in the picture, only the impressions that others have made upon her, Annie D, as on a sensitive photographic plate. Nor is there a world beyond the space within the castle walls, no rest-of-the-world in that summer of '58.

My memory retains no trace of world events, reduced to a distant rumble that reached the camp by way of the television set in the dining hall. The sole exception is the referendum on the constitution announced by de Gaulle, the news of which had deeply shaken the teachers who were communist—partisans of the "No" vote—and sparked debates that Annie D must have watched in silence, instead of taking part. And as concrete evidence of the "events" in Algeria, there are only the airmail letters the cook sets next to the blonde's plate each day at lunchtime. I don't believe the boys ever mentioned the constant threat they faced, from which none were exempt, of being sent to fight in the djebel, in Algeria. Maybe they believed "the revolt" would be "subdued" by the time they were called to serve their country.

On the Internet, I read the list of terrorist actions that occur almost daily between late August (fifteen attacks on the 25th) and the end of September 1958: an attack against Jacques Soustelle that killed one passerby and wounded three, the sabotage of railways, machine-gun attacks on cafés and police stations, fires at factories (Simca in Poissy, Pechiney in Grenoble) and refineries (Notre-Dame-de-Gravenchon-Marseilles).

Apparently, most were reported in the papers (*Le Monde, Le Figaro, L'Humanité, Combat*) but not on television. All were perpetrated by the FLN, which brought the conflict to metropolitan France. The reactions: On August 27, "Michel Debré Introduces Curfews for North Africans," and on August 28, "Raids in the Muslim Circles of Paris: 3,000 Rounded Up for Questioning in the Vélodrome d'Hiver."

None of these facts stir even the faintest memory. What today would be considered a climate of war seemed not to have troubled the girl of S, who I am certain was in favor of "the operations for the maintenance of order" in an Algeria that de Gaulle promised was to remain French. Either she had grown accustomed to the conflict over the three years it had endured, or she labored under a hazy misconception, tinged with romanticism, about death in a distant land, a kind of death that was and always had been a male affair.

Perhaps as a result of that blindness to everything that was not the camp, I come to an abrupt halt when my eye is caught by the date of 1958 in a book or newspaper. I become, once again, a contemporary of events experienced by other people, strangers. I am reunited with a world held in common, and it is as if the reality of others vouched for the reality of the girl of '58.

On September 11, 2001, in Venice, on the Campo San Stefano, along the Rio dei Mendicanti, on the Fondamento Nuevo—a journey reconstructed after the fact—I undoubtedly thought of September 11, 1958, the crowning ritual of my madness, the anniversary which the collapse of the towers in Manhattan will not eclipse, though that event is linked in my mind (at a distance of forty-three years) with the night in 1958 when H, without knowing it then or ever after, became my first lover.

No part of that evening and night of September 11–12 remains in my memory, I realize, other than the circumstances—which must have seemed miraculous, the sign of something fated to be—and several floating images which all thought has deserted, as if desire, in becoming reality, obscured everything that was not itself. And so I have no way of knowing when exactly I learned that H had organized a fondue party to celebrate his departure the following day, and that the blonde, on leave in Caen, would not be there.

The girl in the first image I see hovers excitedly with others around a cauldron bubbling on a hot plate. I imagine her with her stomach in knots and madly hoping, maybe even praying, that her hour of glory has come at last. At the moment when the broomstick taps in the darkened room to prompt a change of partners, and she finds herself in the arms of H, who yanks her dress up and shoves his hand brutally inside her underwear, at that moment a wild joy sweeps through her: she is ravished beyond imagining by a gesture she has yearned for since the first night, three weeks before. There is no sense of degradation, no room for anything but raw desire, chemically pure, as frenzied as the drive to rape, this desire for H to possess her, take her virginity. He tells her—a request or an order?—to follow him to his room. Everything works to the advantage of her desire, even the Ogino calendar, as she has no doubt calculated. Everything flows from her will and full awareness of what lies ahead. It is a night desired, not simply endured like the one of three weeks earlier.

In the second image, I see her on the bed, on her back, legs apart, and trying not to cry out as he thrusts. (What was the thirteenth labor of Hercules? Perhaps this riddle pops into her head.) There has been no foreplay, an alien concept: he thrusts in vain. Maybe he repeats, "I'm too big," after the fellatio she performs of her own free will.

I see him sprawled on his back, and her taking in the sight of him, *naked, sated*, as I wrote in my journal, words which, on rereading them ten years later, I labeled "cheap literature," as I recall. He is unconcerned with her lack of pleasure, tells her that often women do not climax until after giving birth. She must have mentioned the blond instructor because he shows her a framed picture of a pretty smiling brown-haired girl on his nightstand: "There is only one girl I love, and that's my fiancée." A virgin, he adds. He says he always falls in love with the girls he deflowers. She understands that she is not the kind of virgin he could fall in love with, or maybe, all things considered, he is just as happy to have been unable to deflower her. It's all the same to him—six of one, half a dozen of the other. She does not feel humiliated. He tells her to go back to her room because he needs to sleep, he's leaving early. He promises to come and say goodbye at six in the morning. The night of September 11–12 has lasted about an hour and a half.

She does not want to go to bed, must not be asleep when he stops by at dawn. Her roommate is on dorm duty, and she is alone. She discovers streaks of blood in the crotch of her underwear, and her joy knows no bounds. She decides that her hymen has been torn—H has deflowered her after all, even without penetration. The precious blood, the proof, the scar, must be carefully preserved. She will stow it in the closet, under a pile of clothes. And so begins the postlude to the abbreviated night, the sweet night of the imagination. This time H is her lover, truly and for all eternity. Joy and peace prevail, the gift of self accomplished. Heaven and earth will fade away, but this night will remain, her Pascalian night of fire (but who has not had one like it?). No words but those of a mystical variety can possibly transcribe what the girl of S feels. Only in a kind of novel now become unreadable, women's-magazine serials of the fifties, rather than the works of Colette or Sagan, can we touch the immensity, the immeasurable significance, of the loss of one's virginity, the irreversibility of the event.

At dawn, when he does not come to her room, she goes to his and knocks on the door. Silence. She thinks he must still be sleeping. She returns several times (I've forgotten how many). The last time, after knocking, she tries the door. It is bolted. She looks through the keyhole. He is directly in her field of vision with his back to her, in pajamas, stretching. He does not answer the door.

Even if it had crossed her mind (and I think it probably did) that by promising to come and say goodbye, he was simply trying to shake her off, no objective sign of reality— the fiancée, the unkept promise, the lack of a meeting arranged for later in Rouen—can possibly compete with the novel that wrote itself in a single night, in the spirit of Lamartine's *The Lake*, or Musset's *Nights*, or the happy ending of the film *The Proud and the Beautiful*, with Gérard Philipe and Michèle Morgan running toward each other, or the songs (that Esperanto of love) I can list without a second thought:

> *Un jour tu verras / On se rencontrera*—One day you'll see / we will meet again (Mouloudji)

> *Je t'attendrai le jour et la nuit / j'attendrai toujours / Ton retour*—I will wait day and night / always wait for your return (Lucienne Delyle)

> *Si tu m'aimes / Je me fous du monde entier*—If you love me, / the rest of the world can go hang (Édith Piaf)

> *Mon histoire, c'est l'histoire d'un amour*—My story is a story of love (Dalida)

*C'était hier, ce matin-là / C'était hier et c'est loin
déjà*—That morning was yesterday, / yesterday and
already long ago (Henri Salvador)

At this very moment, out in the streets, the open
spaces, on the metro, in lecture halls, and inside millions
of heads, millions of novels are being written chapter by
chapter, erased and revised, and all of them die as a result of
becoming, or not becoming, reality.

When, in the subway or the RER, I hear the first notes
of Dalida's "Histoire d'un amour," sometimes sung in
Spanish, within a second I am emptied of myself, hollowed
out. I used to believe (Proust had a comparable experience)
that for three minutes, I truly became the girl of S. But it is
not she who suddenly revives but the reality of her dream,
the powerful reality of her dream, spread throughout the
universe by the words sung by Dalida and Darío Moreno,
and covered up again, buried by the shame of having had
that dream.

I typed his name into the white pages on the Internet for
the department of Doubs. His surname came up, but with
another given name. After a moment's uncertainty, following
the directory's advice, I extended my search to a neighboring
department. The first and last names appeared, listed at an
address in a village or town I didn't know, probably small.

There was a phone number, too. I sat incredulous before the screen, staring at the letters of the name I had not seen written anywhere for fifty years. To hear the voice last heard in September 1958, the real voice, all I had to do was dial the number. The simplicity of the act seemed frightening. To imagine myself actually dialing the number filled me with the same kind of terror I had felt, sometimes, in the months after my mother died, at the thought that I might hear her voice when I answered the phone. It was as if I would be crossing a forbidden boundary, and at the very moment I heard his voice, the interval of fifty years would dissolve. I would be the girl of '58 again. The feeling I had was a mixture of dread and desire, as if I were about to see a medium invoke spirits of the dead.

Afterwards it crossed my mind that I would probably not recognize the voice of H, just as I had failed to identify that of my ex-husband when I heard it in a video after fifteen years. Or that it might leave me completely indifferent. The power I assigned to this voice to transmute my being of today into the being of '58 was a sort of mystical illusion, a belief that I could effortlessly, through a miraculous short-circuit in time, make my way back to the girl of '58. In the end, by calling H, I faced the possibility of disappointment rather than any kind of danger.

After the night of September 11, she continues to associate with the group but now she is untouchable. They know nothing about her dream. It matters little that H has made no plans to meet her in Rouen. She is sure to find him again in October just by wandering the streets after class at the Lycée Jeanne-d'Arc, where she is about to begin studies in philosophy. She has no leads, apart from the fact that he teaches physical education at a boys' technical college on the left bank.

Few images remain of the last two weeks at camp. It could be that my dream was so unyielding and so meager that reality was unable to take root in memory. One free afternoon, she sits on a boulder high above a sort of lake surrounded by red rock. It is an abandoned quarry, filled with water, deep in the forest near S. She hitched a ride, then hiked down a path littered with stones, leaving the road far behind, and suddenly arrived at this opening, not unlike a canyon. Some teenagers arrived, laid their bikes on the ground, and played in the water. They must have said hello and she not replied because they called, "You're not much to look at, so can't you at least be nice?" This upsets her more than the taunts of the group at camp.

She eats more and more, taking unrestrained advantage of the abundantly available food. The pleasure she finds in eating has become a vital necessity. When no one is looking, she bolts down sliced tomatoes straight from a big salad bowl, prepared for the children in the infirmary. All the freedom she dreamt of in Yvetot becomes reality in her jaunts to the pastry shop in S to buy mocha cream cakes and coffee éclairs.

A summer, autumn, and winter have passed since I returned the girl who was me, Annie D, to the pavement in front of the train station of S, in the Orne. All this time, I've remained within the confines of the camp, forbidding myself to step outside the limits of the summer of '58, either forward or backward in time, forcing myself to remain there, immersed, without a future. As a result, I have progressed very slowly, spinning out those six weeks at camp over some forty other weeks, 273 days to be exact, in order to examine them as closely as possible and make them truly live through writing, that is, to make one feel the immense depth and breadth of a summer of youth in the two hours it takes to read one hundred pages.

Often, I am seized by the thought that I could die at the end of my book. I do not know what this means, whether it is a fear of publication or a sense of completion. I do not envy those who write and never think they could die once the book is finished.

Before leaving S, I pause on the last image, after the children have boarded the buses for the train station, and the silence of the first day abruptly returns, descending upon the space within the castle walls, and she walks to the center of the city to see everything again. She stands alone by the old washhouse, her eyes fixed upon the long façade of the sanatorium in the glow of the five o'clock sun on the other side of the river. She looks at the place where she is sure she has never been happier, not since the day she was born. Where she discovered parties, freedom, male bodies. She would like not to have to go. But everyone has left, or is in the midst of leaving, anxious to be home again. (I may have been the only one who wanted this life to last forever.) It is by no means certain, at this moment, that the hope of finding H in Rouen can make up for the emptiness she feels now. How could one live apart from the companions of summer for a whole year?

But I know that the girl who stands weeping at the edge of the river Orne, devouring a cream cake, is proud of what she has been through, and considers the indignities and insults negligible. She is edified by the pride of experience, the possession of new knowledge whose effect on her in the months ahead she cannot yet assess or imagine. One cannot see the future of something learned.

She did not meet her peers, and she is the one who is no longer the same.

This time—April 28, 2015—I am leaving the camp for good. Until I had returned there, through writing, and remained for months and months, I had not really left. I had not yet risen from the bed where I lay naked and shivering, summarily gagged by the sex of a man for whom, by the next day, I had sworn mad, undying love, leading me to write in 2001: "There is absolute continuity between the room in S and the abortionist's room on rue Cardinet. I move from one room to the other, and what lies between is erased."

It seems to me that I have finally freed the girl of '58, broken the spell that kept her prisoner for over fifty years in that majestic old building on the river Orne, bursting at the seams with children chanting, "We are the band of summer's children!"

I can say: she is me and I am her.

Impossible to stop here. I cannot stop until I've reached a certain point in the past, which right now is the future of my story. I need to reach the time beyond the two years following the camp at S. As I sit with this page before me, those years are not the past for me but, on some deep level, if not literally, my future.

It is a black-and-white photo with serrated edges, two inches square. From right to left, aligned against a partition wall with vertical slats, is a bed with metal bars, a small wooden table pushed against it (rectangular with a drawer), and a closed door with a high window, through which the room's interior can be viewed from the hall.

In the very center of the photo, above the table, a sleeveless summer dress hangs against the partition wall, its armholes looped over two white enamel balls used as clothes hooks. It is a dress with a busy, bright print, flowers or arabesques, and gathered at the waist with a multitude of small tucks, indicating a very full skirt. The light falls on the dress, whose hem brushes against the table, where two books—or notebooks—lie open next to sheets of loose-leaf paper and a pen case. The glaring light is bright enough to bleach the door a dazzling white, emphasizing the smudges of grime above the handle and a mark left by the removal of what appears to have been a lock. In shadow, at the head of the bed, only half of which appears in the frame, is a pale mound of tangled clothes, probably pajamas or a nightgown, and over the headboard, tacked or glued to the partition, is a little picture, out of focus but most certainly religious in nature.

The empty dress stretched over the balls of the clothes hooks, which make one think of the white eyes of a blind person, but enlarged, is eerie-looking—a kind of headless creature dangling from a dubious backdrop. At the same time, there is something luxurious about the dress in its stark environment. (For a moment I feel as if I am about to slip it on, smooth it down over the kind of hooped and ruffled petticoat that gave dresses the bounce and fullness of a crinoline, like the woman's skirt that Belmondo lifts in *Breathless*, and slide my feet into the matching linden-green pumps from Éram.)

The photo has no depth. One has an impression of flatness, as before a painting with no relief. The narrowness of the cubicle and lack of wide-angle lens made it impossible to capture anything but the partition wall, the only sunny spot in the room. On the back of the photo, written in blue felt marker, is the inscription: *Dormitory cubicle in Ernemont before leaving it, June 1959.*

I took the photo after sitting the written exam in philosophy. I had only recently acquired the camera, a Kodak Brownie Flash in Bakelite, given to my parents by a wholesaler. As shopkeepers, they received all manner of gifts when they bought in large quantities. I remember moving the table from under the window, where it usually stood, and pushing it against the bed, as it appears in the photo.

I do not know what it meant to me to photograph the room. It is something I did not do again in the next forty years, or even think of doing. Perhaps I wanted to keep a record of a time of misfortune and metamorphosis, symbolized, it seems to me now, by the two objects in the center of the photo: the dress I had worn most often the previous summer at the camp, and the table where I had spent so many hours toiling away at philosophy.

I examine the photo with a magnifying glass, trying to uncover additional details. I gaze at the folds of the hanging dress, the metal button for the light at the end of a black cable running down the side of the doorframe, a kind that has not been in use for many years. The button replaced an earlier one, which has left a mark above. I am not trying to remember; I am trying to *be inside* this cubicle in the girls' dorm, taking a photo. To be *there* at that very instant, without spilling over into the before or after. To be in the pure immanence of a moment in which I am a girl of nearly nineteen, taking a photo of a place she knows she's about to leave forever. When I gaze intently at the door bathed in white light, a flood of auditory sensations is unleashed. The hourly pealing of the bell, the sharp clap of hands that woke us up at half past six as the dormitory warden made her rounds (a girl from a poor family employed by the nuns), her "Hail Mary, full of grace" echoed in sleepy murmurs that rose from the cubicles (but not mine). The creak of the floor in front of my cubicle, the footfalls of a girl coming in from class, the bang of her door that makes the whole partition shudder, a song she sings to herself as she puts away her things. *Gardez vos joies, gardez vos peines. / Qui sait quand les bateaux reviennent. / Amour perdu ne revient jamais plus.** That is when I'm truly *there*, plunged into the same desolation and expectation, or rather the sensation of something impossible to put into words, as if the fact of being there again put an end to language.

This room is the real that resists, whose existence I have no means of conveying except by exhausting it with words.

I wonder if, perhaps, by gazing interminably at this photo, I did not so much wish to become the girl of 1959 again as to capture the very peculiar sensation of a present that is different from the one I am truly living, sitting at my desk by the window. A *present anterior*, a fragile, maybe pointless triumph, but one which seems to me an extension of our powers of thought and mastery of our lives.

As I write, someone I cannot call *myself* fills the room in Ernemont, someone reduced to pure watching and listening, while the body is nothing but a blur.

The paradox is that I would never want to go back to being the person I was in that room—something quite terrible even to imagine—between the summer of '59 and the fall of '60, in the very thick of the disaster.

---

* "Hold on to your joys, hold on to your pain. / No one knows when the boats will come again. / Love lost can never be regained."

The girl who arrives with her mother on September 30, 1958, in the late afternoon, in this cubicle in the young ladies' hall of residence in the Convent of Ernemont, on a street of the same name in Rouen, is nonetheless eagerly, confusedly, looking forward to a life that will continue the one she had at the camp in S, but in another form. With money the girl earned at S, her mother buys the blanket and bedspread the girl needs for her move into the residence. After her mother has left, the girl knocks at the cubicle next door and heartily greets a small, curly-haired brunette who looks at her, surprised and embarrassed. "Hi, my name's Annie, what's yours?" This will be their sole exchange because her neighbor is an apprentice hairdresser, and the "hairdressing girls," who are in the majority at the dorm, do not mingle with lycée and university girls, and eat at separate tables in the refectory.

She needs other people more than ever, in order to work herself into the state of euphoria she experiences when telling stories about her holiday.

On the first nights, she asks the other girls riddles she learned at the camp, tells the "perfection for a nun" joke,*

---

* *La comble de la religieuse est de vivre en vierge et de mourir en sainte*—literally, "Perfection for a nun is to live as a virgin and die as a saint." When the phrase is spoken, the word *enceinte*, as a homonym of *en sainte*, alters the meaning to "Perfection for a nun is to live as a virgin and die pregnant."

sings raunchy songs like "Maman, what's a virginity?" and "The Museum of Father Plato." She is unconcerned about the others' reserve, which she believes is caused by envy or admiration, until one girl calmly declares that none of her friends use such language. (The girl, Marie-Annick, a former student of the Dominican sisters, daughter of an industrialist, went to fencing class each week and must have despised me even more than I did her.)

The girl writes a warm, nostalgic letter to her former roommate Jeannie, and another to Claudine, the girl with the port-wine stain, who lives in Rouen, and asks to see her. Neither will reply. Did I suspect at that time that they both took me for a brainless little slut?

At the Lycée Jeanne-d'Arc, which she has fantasized about since her school days at Saint-Michel d'Yvetot, she does not know a single one of her twenty-six classmates, and none of the teachers know her. Here, Annie Duchesne wears no halo of past academic excellence. Amidst the other girls, bound to each other, thick as thieves, she discovers she is nameless, invisible. The obtrusive surveillance of the nuns at Yvetot has been replaced by the indifference of the relatively young and elegant professors, whose obvious competence dazzles her as much as it causes her to worry about her ability to keep apace.

In English class, she lives in terror of being asked a question, which she would not even understand the meaning of. The much-anticipated pleasure of physical education and going to the pool comes to nothing. Gym class bores her and pool hours are for girls who already know how to swim. Soon she will ask for a doctor's note to be excused from phys ed.

Contrary to her previous belief, insubordinate dev-il-may-care girls are nowhere to be found. Boys do not throng outside the lycée gates waiting for them on rue Saint-Patrice. She tries to locate the most easygoing girls, but when she does, dares not approach them.

At the convent school in Yvetot, she had been aware of differences in social standing, but the shopkeepers' daughter could boast of grades far superior to those of the rich girls, whose academic performance was often quite the reverse of their parents' social status. At the lycée, she can guess at social disparities beneath the uniformity of the smocks (beige or pink, depending on the week) but cannot clearly identify them.

She feels herself immersed in an atmosphere of supe-riority—impalpable, intimidating. While accepting it as natural, she quickly identifies its source as the parents' pro-fessions (headmaster, doctor, chemist, administrator at the École normale, professors, schoolmasters), their homes in the genteel neighborhoods of Rouen. This superiority is pointedly displayed in the knowing smiles provoked by the diction of Colette P, a mason's daughter, the only girl in the class from a workingman's family, a scholarship student whom a haughty classmate informs one day, with an exasperated shrug, that the verb *to disremember* "is not proper French." The girl is ashamed for Colette and ashamed for herself because for quite a long time, she too had used the word "disremember."

She is a spectator, observes the others' lightness and naturalness when making declarations like "As Bergson says . . ." and "Next year I'm starting Sciences-Po," or "I'm going into *hypokhâgne*"* (she doesn't know what either means). She is an outsider, as in the novel by Camus she reads in October, galumphing, moist and sticky amidst the pink-smocked girls, their well-bred innocence and unsullied sexes.

Her first essay subject in philosophy casts her into a nameless anguish: *Can a distinction be made between an objective and a subjective mode of knowledge?* The girl who in former years wrote essays with ease now becomes obsessed with a task that seems to her sheer terror. She is seized with panic at her inability to find and develop ideas. She wonders if she is unfit to study, or if she should go into law, of which she has heard people say, "It's all memorization." (At this time of my life, I set great store by everything I hear outside of my home environment.)

To write on the subject she has been assigned, she would have to wrench herself away from the camp, the memories

---

* *Hypokhâgne*: preparatory class for advanced studies in arts and literature at the *École normale supérieure*, followed by the *khâgne*. Both are informal, pseudo-Greek expressions, based on the word *cagneux*, meaning "knock-kneed."

of parties and the night of September 11. Erase the imprint a male body has left on her own. Cease to know what a man's sex is. She will manage to submit her paper at the cost of efforts that still seem horrifying to me today. She will even pass, obtain the average mark. She is in a state of unspeakable lack.

The immensity and violence of this lack are brought home by the memory of my shock, one afternoon at the Omnia cinema, where Louis Malle's *The Lovers* was playing. "It was as if he had been expecting her" . . . from the moment these words were spoken, the first measures of the music by Brahms, the woman in the bed ceased to be Jeanne Moreau and became the girl, with H. She is wracked with pain and desire with every image. She is in the cave and cannot get back to herself, reunite with her body on the screen, lose herself in the film's story, which in turn trains a light on hers with H, a light which, even as I write this, I cannot say has altogether died, after all the years it has traveled. The same light is projected on her love by the poems she reads at the time from volumes borrowed from the Capucins Library, every single one she can find from the series *Poètes d'aujourd'hui*. She transcribes lengthy passages from *Poems to Lou* (Apollinaire), from Éluard, Tristan Derème, Philippe Soupault, etc. (Rereading them in the red diary, I realize that I know them by heart: *Sais-je, mon cher amour, si tu m'aimes encore? / Les trompettes du soir gémissent lentement.*[*])

---

[*] "Do I know, my beloved, if you still love me? / The horns of evening play their slow lament."

Sometimes, I raise my head from the page and emerge from the inward gaze that renders me indifferent to my surroundings. I see myself as someone might from the narrow path that runs along a stand of fir trees up above, someone who sees me at the little desk by the window, lit by a big lamp. It is a conventional image, of general appeal (I have often been asked to pose this way for newspapers or television). I wonder what it means for a woman to pore over scenes that happened over fifty years earlier, to which her memory can add nothing new at all. What is the belief that drives her, if not that memory is a form of knowledge? And what desire that exceeds the desire to understand fuels the relentless determination to find, among thousands of nouns, verbs, and adjectives, those that will provide the certainty (the illusion) of having attained the greatest possible measure of reality? What compels her is the hope of discovering even a drop of likeness between this girl, Annie Duchesne, and any other being.

I may agree to question the reliability of memory, even the most implacable, in capturing a past reality, but the fact remains: I seize the reality of my experience at S through the ways in which it affected my body.

My period stopped in October.

Despite her ignorance of the reproductive system and its functioning, the girl of '58 knows enough to be sure she isn't pregnant—she's gotten her period since H left—but can think of no other reason why her blood should cease to flow.

It is a Saturday at the end of October. I see her lying on her parents' bed, next to the unused fireplace beneath a large framed painting of Saint Thérèse de Lisieux. Dr. B, the family physician, palpates and listens to her belly, while her mother stares from her station at the end of the bed. All the actors in the scene are speechless, absorbed. A deathly silence hangs over the room, pending the verdict. The power of the scene, played out for decades in bedrooms and doctors' offices, is equal to that of a timeless painting such as Millet's *Angelus*. The scene in the bedroom and Millet's painting merge, perhaps because of the bent heads: Dr. B's, my mother's. I don't know what the girl is thinking—perhaps she is pleading with the saint over the fireplace. Dr. B looks up again, suddenly talkative, as if anxious to convince the mother of the daughter's innocence. He explains that amenorrhea, "for that is what it is called, madam," is by no means uncommon! He knew of prisoners' wives who went unvisited by a single period for the entire war! The atmosphere of general relief is almost joyful. All that has been imagined but at no moment expressed vanishes into thin air. Tragedy has passed them by. The sister from the Order of the Divine Compassion will come on Saturday to give the girl an injection upon her return from the lycée in Rouen.

For two years no cure can be found for the drying of my ovaries, not the Equanil tablets prescribed by the neurologist, nor the iodine drops prescribed by the gynecologist. I am towed off to one specialist after another by my aggravated mother ("Don't tell me you're going to stay like this forever!"), whose true suspicions are revealed in an astounding piece of blackmail: "You won't be going to the School of Agriculture ball unless you get your period!"

I don't think she believed me innocent. For her, whatever the cause, the absence of periods was a sign of obscure guilt somehow linked to the summer camp: as you sow, so shall you reap. As if it were a shameful defect, neither of us spoke of it to anyone.

Excluded from the community of girls where the cessation of monthly bleeding is unimaginable, barring "misfortune" or far-distant menopause, a step away from death; deprived of this not-especially-welcome monthly visitor, whose arrival girls announced to each other with "My Aunt Rose is here" or "The English have landed," I stood outside of time—ageless.

In October 1958, Billie Holiday sings at the Monterey in Paris, and on November 12 at the Olympia in a concert organized by Frank Ténot and Daniel Filipacchi. She will stay in Paris, at the Mars Club, until the end of the month. She is in a pitiful state, ravaged by alcohol and drugs.

On July 20, 1958, Violette Leduc meets René Gallet,

thirty-five, a cement finisher in the building trade. "My first orgasm at fifty, the one that drew me irresistibly into the fold of men and women devoted to each other's pleasure," she writes in *La chasse à l'amour*. In September, she takes René to Honfleur and Étretat. On October 21, she writes to Simone de Beauvoir, "René Gallet did not write, he did not come and what was given to me was taken away immediately. I want to die." She is overwhelmed by pain. Writing again to Simone de Beauvoir, in December: "It is him I long for, and I long for the impossible," and "I will abandon literature." The relationship breaks down little by little until its total collapse in the spring of 1959.

Reading these things, I am deeply moved, as if the eighteen-year-old girl walking along the boulevard de l'Yser amidst the roar of the Saint-Romain Fair in the fall of '58, were less alone, less forlorn—saved, in a sense—because these forsaken women, unknown to her then, even by name, had lived in desperate solitude at the same time as her. How strange and sweet is this retrospective consolation, when imagination arrives to soothe the pain of memory, to shatter the singularity and solitude of an experience that is more or less shared by others at about the same time.

Over the past fifty years, I have often pictured myself crossing the Seine at the Corneille bridge and roaming the left bank of Sotteville, under reconstruction, searching for the boys' technical college—perhaps the one that Google designates as the Marcel-Sembat technical lycée—where H taught gym, and which I must have located on the map of Rouen on the post office calendar I used as a desk blotter. But it is an imaginary journey. The girl of '58 never crossed the Seine. I did not want to be caught conspicuously searching for H, nor risk an encounter in which I might have the truth flung in my face, a truth suspected and just as soon dismissed, i.e., that he could not care less about me. I didn't ever want to run into him by chance on my usual route to and from school, between rue Saint-Patrice and Place Beauvoisine, or on a Thursday, my day off, on rue du Gros-Horloge. As long as I did not meet him, my dream remained intact.

Because I thought I saw a resemblance between a monitor at the lycée, a wavy-haired brunette, and the girl in the picture on H's nightstand, I said in a mysterious tone of voice to R, a short chubby girl whom I sat beside in class, "That monitor is my rival."

Some nights, in the bathroom on the landing, outside the dormitory, I stood on top of the toilet seat, and through the ventilation window, which was set at an angle facing the Seine, I watched the lights of Rouen spill down the slope to the left bank. I heard the great rumble of the city, the moan of a foghorn. My first lover was somewhere out there, where the darkness began. I don't think that I was suffering. My dream had taken on a new form, become a horizon—the distant prospect of the following summer at S, where I was sure to be reunited with H.

I typed H's first and last name into Google. Both appeared at the top of the list with a series of six photos. Four showed men of between twenty and thirty: to be eliminated right away. The other two were group photos. I clicked on the one in color to enlarge it. It illustrated an article from a provincial newspaper. The title in big letters over the top read: E and H Celebrate their Golden Wedding Anniversary. It was him—the name of the region and the town left no room for doubt. The photo showed a huge group of guests in four tiered rows, huddled together, presumably to fit everyone in the frame, on a grassy lawn with foliage in the background. The faces were distant, a little blurred. The men of my generation all had white hair. I picked him out in the middle of the group as the one with the most powerful build—broad shoulders, impressive paunch, the look of a patriarch—standing beside a shorter woman, possibly wearing glasses, it was difficult to see. He wore a casual shirt with the collar open. Studying him, I recognized the face, its heavy features, the prominent nose that once made me compare him to Marlon Brando. Now, in the photo, he was the later Brando, the one of *Last Tango in Paris*. I counted forty people of all ages, including children sitting on the ground or held in their parents' arms. Later the image will make me think of a summer camp. According to the article, the couple married in the 1960s, had children, many grandchildren, and even great-grandchildren. A man's life.

Nothing can be realer in itself than this photo, taken less than a year earlier, yet what strikes me most, dumbfounds me, is the unreality of what I see. The unreality of the present, of this rustic family portrait, set alongside the reality of the past, the summer of '58 in S, which I have worked for months to transpose from the state of image and sensation to that of words.

How are we present in the existences of others, their memories, their ways of being, even their acts? There is a staggering imbalance between the influence those two nights with that man have had upon my life, and the nothingness of my presence in his.

I do not envy him: I'm the one who is writing.

Today, after looking at the photo on Google again, I have a vague sense of unease, bordering on discouragement. I suddenly envisage a clan, the mass and solidity of a clan that has grown from a seed that engendered a bloodline and developed over a trajectory of social success, free of untoward events: a story of strength in numbers. I think, "I'm alone and they are EVERYONE," like the narrator in Dostoevsky's *Notes from the Underground*. They appear to create a solid front around him, around the Godfather, allied against an endeavor they know nothing about, against the memory of a time when they did not exist, or a time they've forgotten but which I have not. I have the impression they're accusing me of persisting in my folly of fifty years ago, though in a different form, which consists of sitting down at my table every day to unite with this girl who once was me, to merge with her. I am her ghost, I inhabit her vanished being.

I look at the girl in the black-and-white photo, on the back of which is written: "*Bal de l'École régionale d'Agriculture d'Yvetot, 6-12-58.*" With her considerable height and girth, she looms over the couple to her right, a boy and a girl. All three stand in front of a green plant, some kind of potted palm. Her white dress, whose pleated bodice with straps emphasizes her bosom, flares out from the waist in rows of ruffles, revealing fleshy arms and thick calves. She smiles with her mouth closed because of her crooked teeth. The face is broad, the depthless gaze the product of myopia. The mouth is rouged, the hair short and lightly permed, the kiss curl on the forehead the only detail that connects this girl to the one in the *bac* photo of six months earlier. This print is a copy I was given four years ago by Odile, the girl in the couple whom I am standing next to. I do not know when I destroyed my own copy. Probably long ago, unable to say to myself "That's me" or even "That was me, then," before the image of this girl with the massive body whose age one might have put at twenty-five or thirty, and whose face appears to reflect the ecstasy of S. Or maybe because, while looking at this photo, I remembered that the worst was yet to come.

Last night I dreamt about a big bus full of writers, a lot of writers. It stopped on a street in front of my parents' grocery shop. I got out because it was "my place." I had the key. For a moment I feared the key would not open the door. I knew there was no one home. The wooden shutters for the storefront and the door had been pinned on. To my great relief the key turned in the lock. I entered. Everything was as I remembered it, the semidarkness of Sunday afternoons, when the only light that entered was from the other shop window that gave onto the courtyard, shaded in summer by a bright canvas curtain. When I woke up, I thought that only the being or self from the dream was equal to the task of writing what is going to happen next, but that to write what happens next meant putting myself in a position that defied all common sense, a conundrum.

But what is the point of writing if not to unearth things, or even just one thing that cannot be reduced to any kind of psychological or sociological explanation and is not the result of a preconceived idea or demonstration but a narrative: something that emerges from the creases when a story is unfolded, and can help us understand—endure—events that occur and the things that we do?

A dream as it unfolds cannot be charted. All I know for certain is that when we returned to school in January 1959, the girl of Ernemont's dream changed course. (Perhaps the dream was adjusting itself to a growing sense that I'd behaved like an imbecile with H and did not deserve him.) The girl who would appear at camp the following summer would be new in every respect. Beautiful and brilliant, she would bedazzle him. He would fall instantly in love with her, forgetting the girl passed around from boy to boy between the two nights he, H, had spent with her. In this dream, from her position of superiority, she would keep him at a distance and not immediately respond to his desire. The rejected girl of the previous summer would, for a yet-undetermined time, remain untouchable. (Here, I note the first manifestation of a desire for inaccessibility, which, throughout my love life, has always arrived too late.) To make him like me, love me, I had to radically transform, almost beyond recognition. The dream, once passive, had now become active.

It was a veritable campaign for perfection whose key objectives were listed, point-by-point, in the diary that was destroyed, though all were easily restored to memory for having become reality:

bodily transformations: lose weight, become as blond as the blonde from S

intellectual progress: methodically work at philosophy and other subjects by avoiding evening socializing in the cubicles

make up for ignorance and lack of social skills, learn to swim and dance, or acquire a clear edge over other girls my age by learning to drive and obtaining a driver's license.

This performative list included another essential project: to take the Ceméa progressive education training during the Easter holidays and become an outstanding camp instructor.

This prospective conversion of my entire being, physical, intellectual, and social, had the merit—and objective—of helping me forget the nothingness that lay ahead until the summer, when I was sure to see him again.

By going back over those months in the life of the girl no longer of S but of Ernemont, like a historian with a character from the past, I have faced a constant risk of stumbling into a tangle of factors that affect her behavior at every given moment, as well as a need to question the order in which these factors arose and therefore the order of events in my narrative.

A letter of January 23, 1959, confirms my certainty about the philosophy course, the vital role it played. The teacher was a little woman with jug ears, eyes black and lively as a squirrel's, and a curiously deep, authoritative voice: Madame Berthier (Janine, in fact, but a teacher's given name is taboo, never to be uttered), for whom the girl of Ernemont feels admiration tinged with a vague animosity:

"It's crazy how reasonable one can become under the influence of philosophy. By forcing me to think, repeat, and write, over and over, that other people must not serve as a means but as an end, and that we are rational beings, *ergo* unconsciousness and fatalism are degrading, philosophy has done away with my desire to flirt."

I am struck by this clarity of thought. Descartes, Kant, and the categorical imperative—all of philosophy condemns the conduct of the girl of S. Because it makes no provision for the imperative of "coming, instead of kicking up a fuss," sperm in the mouth, whores around the edges, and periods that stop dead, all philosophy makes her feel ashamed and prompts her, in the same letter, to repudiate the girl of S, once and for all:

"Sometimes it seems it was another girl who lived at S [. . .] and not me."

It is a different kind of shame from that of being the daughter of shop- and café-keepers. It is the shame of having once been proud of being an object of desire. Of having considered her life at camp an emancipation. The shame of *Annie what does your body say*, of *I don't know you from a hole in the wall* and the scene by the bulletin board; the shame of being laughed at, and held in contempt. A girl's shame.

It is also shame of a historical variety, predating by ten years the slogan "My body my rules." Ten years is a very short time in the greater scheme of History, but immense when life is just beginning. It represents thousands of days and hours over which the meaning of things that one has experienced remains unchanged, shameful. A thing experienced in a world that existed before 1968, and condemned by its rules, cannot radically change meaning in another world. It remains a singular sexual event whose shame remains insoluble in the doxa of the new century.

I picture that girl from the winter of 1959, bound by pride to assert her will and fiercely determined to pursue goals that will gradually drive her into the depths of misery—to exercise a sort of unhappy will.

First I turn it loose on my body. Starting in January, at the residence, I ceased to ingest anything but a bowl of coffee and milk in the morning, the single slice of meat served at lunch every day except Friday, when boiled fish was served, and then soup in the evening, followed by a stewed or fresh apple. I replaced the previous months' acute and always too-short-lived pleasure of gorging myself on buttered bread and fried potatoes with that of willful deprivation. Following no one's example but my own, I practiced a form of sacrifice whose tangible and conspicuous symbol was the after-school chocolate bar distributed at lunchtime by the refectory sister. I deposit it untouched next to the others in the drawer, and say I will give it to the children at camp next summer. I reject everything that leads to weight gain, according to the leaflet for the Neo-Antigrès fat-burning pills I buy at the pharmacy on the boulevard de l'Yser. Every refectory meal becomes an adventure from which I emerge with only a distant sense of having eaten, or even hungrier than before, and always triumphant, having foisted on my neighbor my allotted portion of Laughing Cow cheese. I feel the pride of a true fasting champion, sworn over body and soul to a war against fat, seeing victory in the figures I read on the chemist's scale and the skirts that hang slack around my hips.

I had not completely conquered hunger but simply worn it down with schoolwork. All I thought about was food. My whole existence revolved around what I could or could not eat at the next meal, according to the number of calories on my plate. The description of a meal in a novel brings my reading to a shuddering halt as surely as a sexual scene. In the dorm, to hear the rustling of the paper bag from which little V extracts an after-school pastry, and then to imagine her chewing, disrupts my concentration. I hated her. When would I be allowed to have a treat? As if the decision did not depend on me but on my double, my ideal self, with whom I had to become one and the same, whatever the cost, in order to seduce H.

The debacle of the will occurred one Sunday afternoon in March, behind the closed shutters of the grocery shop while my parents were out for their ritual spin around the countryside in the 4CV. Today, it is obvious that it could only have happened there, in the grocery, which, until the day I left for camp, had always been the land of plenty, where everything was there for the taking, making other people's houses seem strange and even sad, with all the food tucked away in a sideboard. In the kingdom of my sugar-filled childhood, every sorrow, every slap my mother let fly ended in the comfort of a biscuit tin or a jar of sweets. I don't know what the girl is thinking when suddenly she loses all control of her desire and lunges (so I imagine) at the cheese and caramels and the madeleines for individual sale to customers. Or maybe she does not think at all. It is a first scene of gluttony, when the conscious mind looks on powerless as frenzied hands snatch and stuff a frenzied mouth with food it scarcely chews, food it engulfs for the pleasure of a body become a bottomless pit. With the onset of nausea, the end comes: despair at the fall from grace, a decision to diet for the whole next week in order to purge every last morsel of the vast quantity of food consumed in half an hour. To deliver myself of the burden of my wrongs.

That day, the girl in the grocery shop does not know that she has entered a vicious cycle of drastic self-denial followed by renewed fits of gluttony, triggered by obscure and irrepressible forces. From the very first mouthful of desirable and forbidden food, all resolutions swept away, one must go to the limit of dereliction, eat as much as one can until night, and the next day, at first light, renew the fast: black coffee and nothing else.

She does not know she has succumbed to the saddest of all passions, the passion for food, object of an unremitting, repressed desire that can only be fulfilled through excess and shame. Or that she has begun an infernal alternation between purity and defilement, a struggle whose prospects of victory, over the months ahead, will become increasingly remote. When will I go back to normal, when will I stop *being like this?*

I could not imagine there was a name for my behavior except one I had read in the Larousse dictionary: *Pica*—Depraved appetite. Perversion. I was unaware that such an illness existed. I thought of it as a moral failing. I don't believe I linked it to H.

Twenty years later, at the library, by chance I leaf through a book on nutritional diseases, and am disturbed by what I read. I borrow the book from the library and I am finally able to put a name to the thing that became the backdrop of my life for so many months. Bulimia—an obscenity, that unmentionable pleasure which manufactures fat and excrement to be eliminated, and blood that does not flow. I put a name to that monstrous, desperate form of wanting to live at any price, even that of self-disgust and guilt. Today it is hard to say whether that knowledge, had I possessed it then, could have helped me. Could I have been treated (or agreed to be treated)? If so, how? What could medicine have done to combat a dream?

During that winter of 1959, I picture the girl at the Tarlé dance class, rue de la République, in the evening. She is happy to have been excused from dinner at the dorm. She is disgusted by the dancers' hands, their faces that come too close, their style of humor: *Who's that, just running through the door? —Justin Thyme and Catherine the Late.*

I picture her at the Brasserie Paul, near the cathedral, drinking a cup of Viandox beef broth (considered low-calorie) with R, the only one of her classmates she talks to, a cheerful round-faced girl with faience-blue eyes, who only comes up to her shoulder.

I see the girl in the late afternoon—almost night—on the pavement near the Nouvelles Galeries, watching R's blue wool hat recede into the distance through the window of the bus taking her home to Déville, in the suburbs of Rouen. I know that, at that moment, the girl envies R for not having to go back to the dorm, with its chills and drafts and sounds of bodies taking off shoes, brushing teeth, coughing and snoring. She envies her for not lying awake for hours in the yellowish glare of the night-light in the corridor, which separates her cubicle into two zones, dark and light, whose dividing line cleaves straight down the middle of her bedspread. She envies R for getting to return to a house each night, to her parents' home.

In December she writes to Marie-Claude, "Next year I hope to go to law school, or do a qualifying year of liberal arts. My mother said, though not in so many words, that maybe I could get a room on the university campus, which I would much prefer to a hostel run by nuns. But I'm afraid I'm aiming too high and that it could all fall apart. So these plans strike me as a little utopian. I'm afraid that later I'll regret having had too little education." But in February she applies to take the entrance exams for the École normale for schoolteachers in Rouen. Those who pass the exam are guaranteed one year of professional training after the *bac*.

I have before me Annie Duchesne's school reports for Philo II, 1958–59. They attest to a continuous achievement of good results in every subject, except for English. She finished fifth out of twenty-five in philosophy. Though she is always on the honor roll, the reports contain no words of encouragement or congratulations. The evaluations allude to a "clever and serious student"—a bleak portrait, colorless and flat, consistent with my memory of a girl who never said a word in class. There is no doubt that at the time, as is the case today, these kinds of results qualified a person to plan for long-term studies, so that the girl's desire to join the ranks of the student teachers she'd so admired at S, and to resemble the blonde, seems to me insufficient grounds for her to renounce her earlier ambitions.

I see these months at the lycée as a slow extinction of Annie D's academic ambitions, due to an internalization (without revolt) of her social position, which she is convinced her classmates have not guessed—they were not about to hunt down her parents' café-grocery in Yvetot—though they must naturally have perceived it. At the lycée, surrounded by unabashed "whiz kids" who dared to ask questions of the teachers, her status as "the exception," a sort of miracle case, has lost its power and its value. The academic heroine is no more. She is caught off-balance by the self-assurance of the other girls, who, indifferent to the results of their *bac*—a simple formality—announce that they are going into *hypo-khâgne*, or to study pharmacy, as if their places were already reserved, or Langues O, or Sciences-Po. To her, long-term study now seems an endless tunnel, a sad, exhausting, endless, and impoverished time that will cost her parents dearly while keeping her dependent on them. Advanced studies have ceased to be the source of the happiness she had hoped for, as if everything she'd heard throughout childhood about the "mental exertion" of studying, the freakishness of being "gifted" in the midst of people who went to "the school of the Twelfth of Never" as they said, has finally caught up with her. Now she aspires to the future mapped out by society and National Education in 1959 for talented children of the peasantry, workers, and bistro owners. The girl has fallen back on the father's side of the tree. Before the mother's disappointment, he exults upon learning that his daughter no longer wants to "go further," and hopes to enter the *École* normale (there is no need to add "for schoolteachers," for neither he nor she is aware of the existence of the *École* normale supérieure in Paris—and indeed, who is aware of it today, other than teachers and the elite?).

I also suspect her change in plans has something to do with a question she asks herself: Who wants to sit at a little desk scribbling away like a schoolgirl, when she has the sexual experience of a woman, repressed and denied though it may be?

In the enchanted vision of the future that she entertains at the time, she teaches at a country school, surrounded by towers of books, with a 2CV or a 4CV parked in front of the lodgings that come with the job. She will teach students poems, Francis Jammes's *I love the gentle donkey / Trotting along the hedges of holly*, *The Djinns* by Victor Hugo. In her vision of the teaching profession, the children are present in the blurred and joyful form of those of S, *the band of summer's children*, with whom she had not had to concern herself for more than a week.

As if language, a late arrival in human evolution, did not impress itself as readily as images, all that remains of the thousands of words exchanged with other instructors-in-training at the course held in a castle in Hautot-sur-Seine, during the Easter holidays, is one snickering comment made by a teacher with pitted skin and dark glasses, in the kitchen, where we were teamed up for dish duty: *You look like a decrepit old whore.* I attributed the comment to the excess of foundation and rouge on my pale skin, and was unable to think of any reply but: *And you look like an old pimp*, flustered and probably stunned by the untoward resurgence of the whore around the edges. Was the girl from the summer camp showing through the girl of the instructors' course, whom I believed to be so dignified and cold?

I must have thought with horror that she was about to resurface when, toward the end of the training, weary of the advances of a boy who sat at my table, I allowed him to kiss me and caress my chest in an almost empty cinema, where a B movie full of monsters was playing. Everything inside me pricks up, comes alive against my will, with a terrified awareness of the power of desire, aroused by the hand and mouth of this tall, frail boy. He accompanies me to the door of the hostel and I am sure I will never agree to see him again. In 2000, I received a letter from him through my publisher. He wrote that he had never forgotten "the beautiful girl" of Hautot-sur-Seine—a description that astonished me. He was married with children and ran a garage in Rouen. I do not remember how he had recognized Annie Duchesne, the girl from the training course, in the woman who had just written *Happening*.

One day in April, at lunchtime, when I saw the letter next to my plate in the refectory, stamped with the return address of the sanatorium of S, I may have anticipated the refusal it contained. I do not recall the wording, only its brutal confirmation of my certainty that Annie Duchesne was not wanted at the camp. At that moment, I think, the hardest blow was less the pain of not seeing H again, the definitive end of my dream, but the magnitude of my past indignities, made blindingly obvious by the rejection of my application (it was not unusual for counselors to return to work there two or three years in a row). Clearly no one wanted anything more to do with that girl, at any price, in any capacity. But that was the girl from before. At S they did not know the new girl. The shame was indelible, confined within the walls of the camp.

The inability to situate one memory in relation to another prevents us from establishing a link of cause and effect between the two. I don't know whether I received the letter from the camp before or after reading Simone de Beauvoir's *The Second Sex*. It was the same month, April 1959, and the book belonged to Marie-Claude, from whom I'd asked to borrow it at the end of March.

I will temporarily dismiss the word "revelation," which occurred to me years later on picturing the girl of Ernemont walking to the lycée, completely entranced by the book, awakened to a world stripped of the appearances it had worn only days before—a world in which everything from the cars on the boulevard de l'Yser to the necktied students she meets, walking in the opposite direction toward the École supérieure de Commerce, now signifies the power of men and the alienation of women. For now, I will simply introduce the same girl, with her memories of the previous summer, to a thousand pages of impeccable demonstration, an interpretation of male-female relations which stands to affect her monumentally, as a girl, pages written by a woman philosopher she knows only by name, which propel her into a dialogue she cannot and does not want to evade because there has never been one like it.

I suppose this girl to be:

stunned by the picture it paints of the situation of women, an unhappy epic that has pursued its relentless course since prehistory

overwhelmed by the apocalyptic vision of women ruled by the needs of the species, weighted down by immanence, while men are completely at ease with transcendence

confirmed in her revulsion with regard to motherhood, her fear of childbirth, since reading about Melanie's fate in *Gone with the Wind* at age nine

thunderstruck by the multiplicity of myths surrounding women, and perhaps humiliated by her paltry supply of myths about men, and in any case revolted by the memory of boys at camp who said, *You're the praying mantis type*

astonished by the emphasis the author places on disgust and shame about periods—"the curse"— whereas the cause of her own shame is the absence of blood, her immaculate underclothes.

I do not know whether, in Simone de Beauvoir's dramatic description of the loss of virginity, the girl sees her first night with H, or if she agrees with the statement "The first penetration is always a rape." That I still find it impossible to use the word "rape" with regard to H may mean that she doesn't. And what about the shame of being madly in love and waiting for a man behind a door he did not open, being called *totally deranged* and *a whore around the edges*? Has *The Second Sex* cleansed me of all that, or on the other hand, completely submerged me? I choose not to come down on one side or the other. To have received the key to understanding shame does not give one the power to erase it.

In any case, what matters in April 1959 is the future. I am certain that the philosophy student has answered Simone de Beauvoir's summons on the last page to choose: "I believe that [woman] has the power to choose between the assertion of her transcendence and her alienation as an object." She has received the answer to her question, the one asked by most girls of her time: How am I supposed to *conduct myself*? With freedom.

The girl who leaves Ernemont after photographing her cubicle does not know how to swim or dance, the lessons quickly abandoned, and she has just failed her driving test, but these deletions from her planned repertoire seem to her of little account. She has completed her *baccalauréat* with honors, and I know she is determined more than ever to "fulfill her entire potential" through an altruistic scheme that combines existentialist principles with the ideal of the summer camp: to educate children. She plans to persevere in a direction she believes she has chosen with total liberty.

As I prepare to enter this new summer, dry and burning hot even after the school year starts, which this year for the first time happens in September by decree of General de Gaulle, the summer of 1959, I need to see the girl who for the entire holiday will cease to be Annie D and become Kala-Nag, then Kali, the totemic names by which she was successively known at the camps where she worked that summer. One small, the other medium-sized, the camps were primarily run by women and rigorously proper, unlike the brothel of S, as the girl has come to think of it. I need to see her as she had been readying herself to appear in the eyes of H, and as she appeared to others:

> "the vamp" for Catherine R, director of the
> camp at Clinchamps-sur-Orne, near Caen, who
> took an instant dislike to me, and talked about me
> behind my back one day in the kitchen with the
> other woman counselor—there were two women
> and one man—as I listened from the top of the
> stairs; I do not recall a word of what she said, only
> that I wanted to die on the spot
> "the singular girl" for Lynx, the director of the
> Ymare colony, near Rouen, who with a knowing
> laugh presented me with a novel by Jules Romains
> for my birthday, entitled *A Singular Woman*, and I
> heard him say to his wife, Ant, with another laugh,

"In all the time I've worked at summer camps, I've never had a counselor like Kali!"

Of all the girls above, is she not in fact the one who on 29 July '59 writes a letter she posts in a yellow envelope with the seal of the Federation of Lay Works, Camp Ufoval: "In Caen I saw *Without You, All Is Darkness* with Eva Bartok. That passion for morphine boggles the mind, you start to think it could happen to you, and the idea isn't even shocking."

Even though I had to wear jeans or shorts and sneakers to go on walks with my group, I picture this girl in a dark green dress with a pattern of big lime-tree flowers—the one I am wearing in the only photo I have from the summer of '59, taken on an almost empty beach where I sit amidst the yards and yards of fabric of the skirt, which springs from the waist like a many-petaled corolla. I look like a doll won at the fair on my cushion of smooth flat stones, perched on pumps with stiletto heels, also pale green, from Éram. They raise me to a height of almost five foot eleven. Boys I pass on the street sometimes sneer, "So how's the weather up there?" Yes, things are different for a girl who is tall, whose gaze glides over the heads of most, and with others moves down to the level of their hair, and sweeps all the way to the end of the block. If boys do insult a girl who is tall, they're less likely than with short girls to put their hand on her bum. With her bleached-blond hair pulled back in a chignon on the nape of the neck and covering her ears, in the manner of Mylène Demongeot, and her voluminous skirt, she embodies a conspicuous and untouchable femininity. With her body and her attitude, she enacts a fusion of her affair with H and the injunctions of *The Second Sex*.

Whether as Kala-Nag or Kali, she does not want to be a vamp or "singular," quite the opposite. She longs to conform to the model of the good counselor, as defined by her training program—to be like the others and contribute to the atmosphere of "frank and wholesome camaraderie." So why would she choose the name and emblem of an incendiary goddess like Kali, when the other female instructors abide by the usual rule of flower names, Jasmine, Daisy, etc., if not from a desire to be different? I am unable to assess the extent of her self-delusion. Did she really think she was pulling the wool over their eyes? Concealing her vice, her obsession with food that she declines at mealtimes but greedily eyes on other people's plates, and finally devours at snack time, outdoors with children who are only too happy to give her slabs of bread and butter and quince jellies they do not want for themselves. She must not let show any of the effort she expends to interest herself in the games she painstakingly organizes (the urge to flee is overwhelming, but there is nowhere to go), the sheer torment of inventing a ballet for her twelve girls to perform to music from *The Nutcracker* for the parents, dockworkers in the port of Rouen, who, for the occasion, provide several kilos of bananas, which she gorges herself upon. She must suppress the feeling that her behavior is continually at odds with her surroundings.

Tiny, adorable, curly-haired Violette, who asked me point-blank, What is an unfit mother? Claudette, always on the verge of an explosion, a walking tower of reproach, who pulled me to her violently when I went to kiss her good night. Maryse, who called the other girls "twats" and laughed uncontrollably when scolded for it. The well-behaved brunette with the pageboy haircut who had read *The Little Prince*, etc. In these precise memories of the faces of the ten-to-twelve-year-old girls who were my charges at Ymare, what I perceive most of all is an inability to feel anything for them. As if turned to ice inside, I saw all beings from a distance.

This Kali/Kala-Nag of the summer of '59 is devoid of feeling. She repels the children's shows of affection as something animal, untamed, a breach of the principle of equality. Indifferent to danger, she hitchhikes, or crosses the woods alone to visit a chapel on her day off. She is very nearly bitten by a viper she did not see because she does not wear her glasses. The snake lay coiled a fraction of an inch from her sneaker. She writes, "I didn't know whether I had been bitten . . . The children urged me to go back to camp, but I was in no hurry. Believe it or not, it didn't affect me one way or the other to think I might be in danger of dying."

Her thoughts no longer have an object. She inhabits a world from which all mystery and flavor have disappeared. The real has ceased to resonate inside her except in the form of painful emotions, disproportionate to the cause. She is driven to the verge of tears when she thinks she has lost an unread letter from her mother.

Deep inside, she would have liked to remain an adolescent, as she reveals in a letter about the fourteen-year-old girls at the camp:

"I sincerely envy them. They have no idea that they have the best of everything now. It's stupid not to know when in our lives we'll be happiest."

Self-narrative, in bringing to light a dominant truth that it seeks in order to ensure a continuity of being, always neglects to consider the following: our failure to understand what we experience, at the moment we experience it; the opacity of the present, whereby every sentence and every assertion should be riddled with holes. The girl whom the children call Kali, who trudges along with them down the bumpy country roads singing *The camp we lo-o-o-ve / A blossoming grove*, does not know, cannot put a name to "what the matter is." She just eats.

One afternoon, when there was no one else in the dormitory, she stole sweets from a little girl's locker. The victim's accusations against the other girls in the group were not pursued. Naturally, Kali the counselor is above suspicion. The image remains of an act committed by someone else, a girl in the clutches of an irrepressible impulse. But today I can still see the wooden box above the bed, recall the silence of the dorm. All thought surrounding this image has fallen away. I do not know how many sweets I stole, only that I ate every one of them on the spot.

At the beginning of September, she is summoned to the entrance exam for the BA program at the École normale for schoolteachers in Rouen. She feels she has performed brilliantly in her oral presentation on friendship, but is sure she will fail on account of the drawing test and the written summary on tidal power plants. She is dumbfounded to learn she has ranked second out of sixty-odd candidates for twenty spots, a classification that seems to her an irrefutable sign from destiny.

An image from that September afternoon: sitting on the bed in her room in Yvetot, facing the chest of drawers with the mirror above, listening to a record of Strauss waltzes, a gift from friends of my parents—insipid fare, in my opinion, but at that moment a perfect accompaniment to my sense of triumph. I revel in this moment of pure success with a violence edified by the Viennese music and the sight of my reflection in the mirror, as if it represented the future and the world awaiting my arrival. It is a moment of blindness, has remained the moment of absolute error, a first step in the utterly wrong direction.

On that Sunday night after her arrival at the school, having put away her clothes and other items she had been required to bring, all marked with her initials, before she falls asleep in a bed that seems too short, surrounded by the pink walls of a cubicle, open at the floor and ceiling, like a sort of cozy padded box for a doll, does she feel she has landed in the place she once dreamt of going, back in the days at camp, and that now she too is a student teacher, like the blonde?

My fragmented memories of the École normale—the porch where we entered, the dorm, refectory, courtyard, and gym, etc., the areas I commonly used—are supplemented by the Internet, which provides a stunning panoramic view of the whole. Built in 1886, it covered an area of 23,000 square miles, overlooking Rouen all the way to Côte Sainte-Catherine. There were gardens, a rose nursery, a playing field, an auditorium, a room for music and dance. A glass canopy ran around three sides of the main building's monumental façade, surrounding the schoolyard. Closed in 1990, fallen into disrepair, attacked by dry rot, the building was sold in 2014 by the department of Seine-Maritime for four million euros to the Matmut corporation, which is supposed to turn it into a complex with a four-star hotel, a convention center, a public park, etc. One photo shows the walled windows of the ground floor, the broken windows on the upper floors, the weeds.

The sight does not sadden me in the least.

Before this building becomes a gilded cage, a deadly cocoon that I will leave, suitcase in hand, one sunny Saturday afternoon in February 1960, and in a state of pure bliss walk down the rue du Champ-des-Oiseaux to the station, I easily imagine Annie Duchesne the student teacher's delight at the magnificence of the place, the sumptuous facilities: in short, the perfection of an organization that reminded her of the camp at S, but on a larger scale. No doubt she wrote her parents a detailed report—especially for the sake of her father, to bolster his pleasure in knowing her to be safe from harm in a land of plenty—on the abundance and variety of meals, the petits-beurres served each morning at ten. Central heating in the dorm, all the "benefits" of a free coverage of expenses, from the TB vaccination to the re-soling of shoes, and even the saving of a "nest egg," to be delivered at the end of training. (The memory of this snug and meticulously planned autarky will help me understand the nature of the Soviet system and, later, the nostalgia with which it is still regarded by the Russians.)

It is even possible that as first-time boarder, she initially adapted to the rigorously supervised, insular quality of this exclusively female world (with the exception of the history teacher and Nicolas, the toad-faced handyman), at least until the sight of her neighbor washing her feet each morning, under the partition, concentrates all her sadness and ennui, mixed with revulsion, at the sexual homogeneity, day in, day out and as far as the eye can see. Or until she lifts the lid of the trash in the bathroom and gazes with disgusted fascination at the red-stained towels dropped there by strangers. She has not seen a drop of her own menstrual blood for over a year.

R, too, has passed the exams and been admitted to the École normale, but is allowed to be a day student like some of the other pupils who live in Rouen or in the suburbs. I had met up with her again with the mingled sense of reassurance and sweetness that the presence of a former classmate can provide in an unfamiliar setting. From the start, the shared memories of the earlier class made us fast friends, colluding in our criticisms of our new institution and the other girls.

In a letter to Marie-Claude dated Monday, September 21, after a passage that radiates enthusiasm—"All the girls went to see *Hiroshima mon amour*, and in chorus we repeated, 'You did not see anything in Hiroshima!'"—she airs an early judgment of the school that already reveals a dearth of enthusiasm, even a certain disenchantment: "It's bearable. The courses are varied, psychology, pedagogy, drawing, singing, home economics, and the atmosphere is good. It doesn't seem to be overly tiring. So much the better."

The bright new candidate, Annie D, does not excel in

any of the subjects specifically related to teaching, has no interest in or liking for anything but the courses in twentieth-century literature and contemporary history, which do not count in the final results, and, most of all, the cooking lessons. These consist of preparing entire meals in a superbly equipped kitchen, where she secretly grazes on raisins and candied fruit from the supplies cupboard. Like the other student teachers, she starts to knit, buys big needles and sky-blue mohair wool—currently in vogue—to make herself a thick cardigan, but she gives up after four inches of lumpy stitches.

How does one grasp the state of mind, the view of life, of her life, that of the girl I see in class, slumped in the third row between R and Michèle L, consumed by an obsession with eating, or in a tracksuit and sneakers, giving her first gym lesson to the students of the "demonstration school" next door, wanting only for it to end, in the days before she is able to admit to herself that she has chosen the wrong future?

She represses the frightening, unavowable perception of being unfit to teach primary school, and falling terribly short of the standard the prestigious École normale strives to instill in its students, as if it were incumbent on the schoolmistress to act as moral steward for all of society. How to measure her despair? With the vivid memory of having wanted to be the dinner lady pushing the food cart to the refectory and serving the plates to each table.

What remains of the desire and suffering of the year before? A sharp intake of breath upon seeing the tightly entwined bodies of Emmanuelle Riva and the Japanese man. The violent agitation and a feeling close to nausea when she reads Christiane Rochefort's novel *Warrior's Rest*, as if she were the novel's heroine: that slave.

Filtered by the walls, the outside world has lost its power to engage her. Neither the events in Algeria—which she has taken an interest in since studying philosophy, firmly in favor of independence—nor the deaths of Gérard Philipe and Camus move her. The songs belted out by girls in the dorm who like the sound of their own voices, Piaf's "Milord," Brel's "La valse à mille temps," and Bourvil's "Salade de fruits" grate on her nerves.

The shadowy forms of students slip across the spatiotemporal stage I have fixed myself for this writing—those five months at the École normale in Rouen. More and more appear, as if this purposeful setting of boundaries launched the wide-scale clearance of a memory warehouse sealed for decades. Names and faces return, those of girls I may have wondered about at the time: What were they doing in that place, were they happy to be there, to become primary school teachers?

How did the others see me, the girls in my professional training class—Annette C, from a small village, La Vaupalière; Michèle L from Gravenchon; Annie F from the rue des Arsins, near the ManuFrance store in Rouen? What did they know about me that I did not know they knew? What others believe about us is nothing compared to that which they do not know, and gives them quite a start when they find out, *Who'd have thought . . . ? I never would have guessed*, etc., so why is it important to me today as I write this? Quite simply, it was the basis of my relationship to the world at the time, when we were together, formed a group, the body of future elementary school teachers, which—did they suspect?—I was unable to feel was mine.

"Anyway, that is what I chose, but to say I really chose it is quite another matter, don't you think that, in fact, we are pulled into things by events?" Letter of December 1959.

When I began to write last year, I scarcely imagined that I would linger over my time at the École normale. I realize that I needed to reactivate the girl who had made a commitment (I signed up for ten years) and ill-advisedly strayed into an occupation for which she was not in the least suited, in order to ask a question rarely broached in literature: How does anyone who is just starting out in life muddle through the necessary ordeal of *finding a way to earn a living*, deal with the moment when a choice must be made, and, eventually, with the feeling of being, or not being, where they ought to be?

It is winter. The student teacher who emerges from the Marie-Houdemare Elementary School wants to die or (and this amounts to the same thing) cease to be the girl whom the ideal-schoolmistress, an elderly spinster, has just upbraided, jet-black eyes gazing piercingly into her own (which immediately filled with tears), and harshly declared in front of the other student trainee, *You do not have the calling, you are not cut out to be a teacher*. That the woman has the reputation of a tyrant among the student teachers, and that all of them dread attending her preparatory class, in no way alleviates the horror of what I immediately perceive as the truth. A truth exposed, in spite of myself and my efforts to prepare reading and writing lessons, invent a Christmas tale with drawings of reindeer and a cottage in the snow. What am I to do with the truth that I am useless, inept in my chosen field?

Next I see the girl flee to the nearby Church of Saint-Godard, before returning to the school to be with the other girls, who, quite unlike her, are thrilled to stand before a class of pupils and be allowed to freely circulate in the streets of Rouen.

I will not be saved by the inspection, which takes place in the final days of training, when the inspector, headmistress, and ideal schoolmistress sit in a row on chairs by the window and chat while I hold up a piece of cardboard on which I have written, in giant letters, new words from the reading lesson. The best pupil, whom I question at the end of the lesson, confuses the verb "to have" with the verb "to be," and replies, "The shepherd is a cloak." In her little downcast face, about to dissolve into tears over the error she has committed, I read a painful confirmation of my own worthlessness.

It does not matter that, for years, every time I pictured this icy woman, her strangely wide-set eyes, thin mouth, and elegant teeth, I wanted to knock her down and trample her, and I must admit that by way of her verdict, excruciating at the time it was delivered, she may not exactly have been my salvation, but she certainly saved me a great deal of time. She is one of those beings—not often the most lovable—who have, I believe, in spite of themselves, changed the course of my life.

As for R, she fell ill at an opportune time, just after a failed grammar lesson, and could not finish her training at a suburban school. Was our friendship sealed, when school resumed in January 1960, by our common failure to stand the test of reality in our profession? And was it that which led to the fusion of mind and instinct, an exclusive conspiratorial bond whose founding moment I trace back to the following event: our bee-like foraging in the college co-op's supply of Carambar caramels, lollipops, and BN chocolate biscuits, stored in the classroom next to ours, after which, by tacit agreement, we left without paying? The caper was soon repeated, though more cautiously after the way the co-op manager had carried on upon discovering the theft. We repeated the offense with childish pleasure and no clear awareness that we were trampling on the morals we were meant to transmit to our pupils. Or maybe we were not as unaware as all that.

Am I to suppose that it took us several hours to work each other into a frenzy of daring in the empty rooms we sought for privacy, out of the others' earshot, or did the idea appear all of a sudden, first as a hypothetical possibility and then as a shared plan: leave the École normale, go to England as au pair girls, and then return to study literature in October? Who had the idea first? R, I'll wager. Annie D, whom I see as a hopeless bulimic, mired to the teeth in the torpor of the boarding school, would have been unable, even in imagination, to wriggle free of the trap she had leapt into, or, on the other hand, take the lead in ending a commitment, a process that required the parents to pay for the months we had spent at the school, all of which, in the end, proved astonishingly easy for all concerned, headmistress and parents—something that from the depths of my dereliction I would never have dreamed possible.

The fact that neither of my parents knew the meaning of the "propedeutic," the qualifying year for university in which I would enroll, did not prevent my mother from glowing with pride and ambition, ready to make every sacrifice so that her girl could "rise through the ranks." My father was as disappointed as if I had openly scorned his ideal. (For his entire life, he kept the newspaper clipping from the *Paris-Normandie* noting my success in the entrance exam for the École normale in a fold of his wallet. Nothing would ever deprive him of this moment of greatest happiness, his revenge on the world as a country kid thrown out of school at twelve to work on a farm.)

The limit of my own ambitions, however, is clearly indicated in a letter of February 29, 1960:

"I'd like to be a university professor, but I may not get that far. I'd also like to be a librarian, the return of my old dream."

The end of March 1960. I see her standing in the corridor of a train in the station at Boulogne-sur-Mer. Her hair is blond. She wears gold-rimmed glasses with a black border on top, and a sky-blue three-quarter-length coat, too light for the season, but she had no room in her suitcase for winter clothes, and she'll be back in the autumn. In a few minutes the train will continue to the ferry terminal with the passengers bound for Folkestone. Through the closed window, she looks at her mother, who, having been ordered off the train, stands motionless on the platform, surprised and crushed that she can go no further, cannot accompany her daughter through customs onto the boat. The mother smiles bravely and the girl feels her eyes fill with tears. It is doubtful she remembers the corresponding scene that took place a year and a half earlier, in front of the station of S. It is I, today, who, as I write, draw a parallel between the two scenes, and, remembering those tears, note the disparity between the two girls. The first girl, defiant, could not wait to leave her family and the little town; the second one, stripped of pride and greed, tries to put a brave face on things, overcome the sorrow of departure and separation. That girl wants no part of the unknown that lies ahead. She has never been to Paris, and no doubt already pictures her arrival in London alone, her delivery to the home of a foreign family with whom she is to live for six months, an eternity. It is a far cry from her dreams of childhood and adolescence. She is leaving because she chose the wrong future, an emigrant from the land of failure. It was impossible to "hang around doing nothing" in Yvetot, idle and embarrassing to her parents, who would be pestered by the customers' questions, their malign curiosity. She has to leave, it cannot be avoided, has been ordained since primary school and her first good results there. She must not want, must not choose to stay at the kitchen table with its oilcloth cover, in Yvetot. She must, as her mother says, "move forward." She is Sarah in the Aznavour song that secretly torments her, *We do not live for our parents*. She must cut herself adrift from her only mooring in the world. The prospect of R joining her in London two weeks later is of no help at all.

The first letters to Marie-Claude, with a return address that reads "Miss A. Duchesne, Heathfield, 21 Kenver

Avenue, London N12 England," resonate with an enthu-siasm that disappeared at the time of the camp at S. She is pleased to be staying with people like the Portners, who are "in tune with the times," and who are "throwing a garden party in three weeks." She is pleased the children, Brian, twelve, and Jonathan, eight, do not require much looking after since they are quite grown-up. She describes the house as "very beautiful, with red wall-to-wall carpet and mirrors, a kind of American style." She mentions "their religion, which is Jewish, and the custom of Friday night dinner, with candles on the table." She lists the places she has visited: the National Gallery, "with Manet, Monet, Renoir, *The Source*," St. Paul's Cathedral, the Madame Tus-sauds museum "with the Chamber of Horrors," the Tower of London, the Docks, Buckingham Palace, Marble Arch, Piccadilly Circus. After writing "I love my life, I like to be cosmopolitan, I would like to visit the whole earth and love it all," she adds, with a touch of vanity—and, as the girl who not so long ago had never left her hole, with uncon-scious revenge on her more socially advanced friend: "Back in Yvetot, we might have said that it was you who were des-tined for a life of wandering and me for a settled life, no? Events truly transform us."

I can imagine that by "events" she means the summer camp, H, and her brief time at the teachers college. One thing is certain—this girl who writes with obvious pleasure, "England is the land of tranquility, of established things. The grass is very green, people like pale colors, pink cakes, the songs of crooners like Perry Como," is back inside the world. Though she is still enslaved by her depraved appetite, and her blood does not flow, she is emerging from her ice age.

Years later, when I become more conversant with "good taste," the mainstream variety, the Portners' lacquered, gilded interior, devoid of antique furniture, a library, or books, except for *Reader's Digest*, will seem to me typically *nouveau riche*. But the girl of 1960 must have felt she had arrived in a land of luxury. A sitting room with heavy drapes and two deep pillowy settees face-to-face, a big television set, coffee tables, a liquor cabinet. A kitchen replete with appliances she has never seen outside of store windows, an electric cooker, refrigerator, washing machine, toaster, blender—did she think of Tati's film *Mon Oncle*, which she had seen the year before and which had failed to make her laugh?—and a gleaming pink bathroom, an ivory phone on a carved pedestal in the vestibule. To lie stretched out full-length in a tub for the first time restores her lost delight in the present. And to move, breathe, eat, and sleep in this setting, to acquire the natural use of new objects, helps her to submit without protest to other things she heartily dislikes. Far from simple "domestic help for the lady of the house," as her job was described by "International Relations," the association that administered au pair girls, her new tasks consist of:

every morning, washing the dishes, the kitchen and morning-room floors, scouring the bathroom

and toilet with Ajax, vacuuming all the rooms
(except for the stairs, which are to be dusted with a
hand broom and a dustpan)
    every week: polishing the front door stoop and
the brass, ironing.

This memory, too, is implacable.

In short, this immersion in a higher-ranking social environment made me come to terms with what my father
claimed I had been in England: "basically, a little house-
maid!" This reflection, though he laughed when he said it,
will cut me to the quick, a humiliating truth. Still, I had
availed myself of all the shortcuts spontaneously dictated
by a position of servility: instead of thoroughly airing the
beds, simply pulling up the sheets and blankets, or cleaning
the glass table by spitting on it, all in the name of being free
to do whatever I wanted by lunchtime.

My determination to "achieve a thorough mastery of
English," as I wrote in my letter of introduction, in which
I also claim to read the *Daily Express* and to have started
reading *Chocolates for Breakfast* by "the new Françoise
Sagan," the American author Pamela Moore, and gone to
see *The League of Gentlemen*, swiftly unraveled. The fatal
blow was not so much the difficulty of attending classes
in the suburbs (held only once a week, at night) as the

availability of contemporary French novels at a Finchley lending library. Letters report "remorse for burying myself in French prose," and list the books I've read, all quite recent publications:

La modification, Butor

Le dernier des Justes, André Schwarz-Bart, wonderful

Les mauvais coups, Roger Vailland, stunning!

Au pied du mur, Bernard Privat, liked it

Les amitiés particulières, Roger Peyrefitte, quite dull

Le dîner en ville, Claude Mauriac

Les enfants de New York, Jean Blot

This inability to resist the pleasure of immersion in my own language undoubtedly grew more intense when I found myself constantly steeped in a foreign tongue, everywhere I went. My initial willingness—which could not have been based on deep desire, judging from a memory of stupefaction and horror I felt at the very idea of "thinking in English," as a girl in class claimed to do—totally collapsed with the arrival of R, who was placed with a family who lived just a mile away from mine.

I never finished reading the book by Pamela Moore, who, according to Wikipedia, killed herself in 1964.

I realize that R is my only "friend from youth," a friend from the period just preceding my entry into the bourgeoisie, marriage, and professional life, of whom I possess no photos, apart from the Philo II class photo, taken in October 1958, in which we are two rows apart. She sits in the front row, her hands placed flat on top of one another, on her school smock. In her face—which today, beneath her short dark blond hair, strikes me as strangely moon-like and cold—her lips, unsmiling, are set in a favorite pout I'd often seen, a mixture of derision and self-satisfaction. Seated, she appears taller than she really was—five foot two—and at a closer look, one sees that her legs, stretched out and pressed together, only touch the ground with the tip of her flat-heeled oxfords.

In my memory, it is another R that I see, a decisive little person with expansive gestures, and a face whose expression changed from smiling ingenuity—for the benefit of those she wished to charm, adults of both sexes—to stony fixity. Her voice, nicely modulated, quite deep, would lose its usual peremptory inflection—not without difficulty, it is true—to grow gentle and caressing when her object was to please.

What else can I say about R before I start to make her over as Xavière in Beauvoir's *She Came to Stay*, and can no longer bear her aggressiveness?

> before, when she's invited to my house, in
> speaking to my father, she uses the expression "How's
> it going, sir?" used by those who think themselves

superior, to stoop to the level of their social inferiors (so they believe)

before I realize that she would never invite me to her parents' house so as not to make me ashamed of mine

before I repudiate her, more or less, in the summer of 1961, in a letter written jointly with G, a new friend from university

and before I cease to see her for good, except for one last occasion, in 1971, in the spa park at Saint-Honoré-les-Bains, near the central basin, when I saw her from the back in the company of a man and a little girl, and I recognized her curiously muscular calves, like a cyclist's, and when she turned around our eyes met, and then we looked away without a word exchanged.

What can I say about her, and why say anything?

Perhaps because I cannot resurrect the girl I was in England—and who, for a long time, I call "the London Girl" after the Pierre Mac Orlan song, sung by Germaine Montero, *A rat came into my room*, etc.—independently of the aimless couple we formed, R and I, hitched together under the same yoke to the exclusion of all others, in a foreign country.

Maybe quote what I wrote to Marie-Claude:

"R [. . .] is a terrific girl, open-minded, a lark, incredibly optimistic, never any problems!"

In this letter of mid-May, six weeks after R's arrival, I perceive my rapt admiration of her way of being in the world, an ease and lightness I do not possess—which was, and still is, the polar opposite of my own way of being. I now attribute this lightness to R's certainty of being "adored" by her parents, who preferred her over an older sister, a married, unemployed mother of two, next to whom R must have seemed the very image of a little genius. I also attribute it to her social milieu, which I did not know much about but which certain details had led me to identify as more well-to-do than my own: a father who worked "in an office" as an industrial designer, a mother who stayed home, holidays on the French Riviera, classical music LPs. Perhaps it was her utter lack of concern about the future, typical of a doted-upon child from a petit bourgeois milieu, which had prompted her to follow me to the École normale and enabled her to come out the other side fresh as a daisy, unscathed.

We spend all of our free time together. When our "ladies"—as we call the housewives for whom we work— are out, we rush to phone each other (telephones in private homes were a great discovery for us both). I picture us, the odd couple, Long & Short, Ole & Axel, at Tally Ho Corner, Finchley's shopping center, tromping to the Woolworth's milk bar and farther afield to Barnet, Highgate, Hendon, Golders Green, as cars whistle by on roads where pedestrians like ourselves are few and far between. We are convinced that with all the miles we walk, we are burning off the pounds we've gained with all the things we eat—lemon curd, shortbreads, trifles, Smarties and Milky Ways, Caramac and Dairy Milk bars, ice cream sandwiches flecked with snowflakes purchased from vending machines for fourpence. We are thrilled by the novelty of these sugary flavors and long to taste them all. I sweep her into my greed. The London Girl has found in R an excellent partner in the dizzy two-step of binge-and-fast.

We talk for hours, nursing a single cup of tea or Bovril beef broth—the English counterpart of Viandox—in Tally Ho's coffeehouse, owned by a bespectacled gray-haired woman who endlessly washes cups and wipes them dry. Our common base of experience, the lycée and the École normale, feeds our conversations. Zealous co-conspirators, we find limitless grounds for criticism, comparison, and denigration in the English way of living and being. We hold forth without lowering our voices, certain we will not be understood if we call someone an asshole or a bitch. We are transplants, roots still dangling, in a giddy French bubble within a society whose rules—whether farcical or not—do not apply to us.

It is only for R that I am Annie. The rest of the time, the Portners' pronunciation transforms my name into "any": indefinite, signifying one, some, or all indiscriminately, of whatever kind or quantity.

We keenly savor the break with the immediate past, the École normale that we revile with all our might, unconcerned about a nebulous future that will only start in October, at university. I see us dwelling within a vacuous freedom. Later, I will think of those months of England as "the Sunday of life which equalizes everything and removes all evil," in the words of Hegel. An English Sunday in 1960, vacant and idle.

There are no flings, no true love on our horizon. This does not seem to worry R, in spite of the desire and satisfaction she feels when she attracts the gaze of men, to whom she responds with an air of naïve bewilderment. Her entire sexual experience amounts to kisses on a beach the summer before. The London Girl feels mature and womanly next to R, who for her is still a little girl. Perhaps it is this supposed innocence (I could not even imagine her masturbating) that prevents the girl from confiding "I had a lover." And, as I more or less believed was the case, "I'm not a virgin anymore." I don't think it weighed on me unduly to maintain a zone of prohibition in our friendship. To do so, indeed, seems to me consistent with my desire to forget H, the summer camp at S, and the shame I had felt, since my year studying philosophy and reading the works of Simone de Beauvoir, at having been a "sex object." We outdid each other in demolishing love and passion: pure alienation, absurd illusion. I wrote in a letter to Marie-Claude:

"We are having a good time without males."

The beginning of this text seems very far away. There is a homological relation between life and writing. My narrative of the first night with H feels as distant now as the real event must have seemed to me in Finchley. These two time spans, now that I think of it, are not so very different from each other. I finished writing about the night of August 1958 thirteen months ago, and at the time I was in Finchley, the night with H was twenty months past. Both these periods of time are at once lived and imagined.

While I am sure of the identity of our desire, I cannot recall the circumstances—the exact place, or day, or the object of our yearning—in which we first reproduced the deeds performed at the École normale co-op. No doubt we were enthralled by the supermarket with its self-service policy, virtually unheard of in France. To conduct our operations in a true retail setting and risk being caught must have unleashed a new and unfamiliar pleasure, enhanced by the voluptuous retelling of our exploits later, sitting in a bar or a park after leaving the store and examining our booty, doubled up with laughter.

At first, our sphere of operations was limited to sweets, for which an elderly tobacconist couple in particular, the Rabbits, paid the price. Their display stand for chocolate bars and rolls of Smarties was level with the opening of my blue-and-white bag, the one I had taken to camp, and I simply shoveled them in. We soon branched out to trinkets from the shelves at Woolworth's—lipstick, nail care, and sewing supplies. Though the paltry wage of an au pair—one and a half pounds a week—did not allow for spending sprees, I was able to buy two dresses during my stay, as well as modest gifts for my parents, and a little valet tray in Wedgwood, very chic at the time, as a parting gift for the Portners. We are not motivated by need or love of ownership, but by the game. The adventure.

It begins at the store entrance with a survey of the premises and the selection of a zone of activity. It is important to maintain a natural appearance while remaining on the lookout. All faculties of attention, imagination, and assessment of others strain toward a single goal: to approach the coveted object, pick it up, set it down, move away, and come back, the choreography improvised one second at a time. The strike is the work of the body, which is transformed into a radar, a keen sensor of the environment. One enters a state of acute self-awareness. The moment of the hit, when the hand makes the object disappear into a pocket or a bag, is charged with an acute consciousness of self, of the danger of being oneself at that moment, which lasts until the falsely casual exit from the store with that burning thing in one's possession. After that, nothing can surpass the jubilation, outside, at fifty yards' remove for safety, of having yet again defied fear, attained a peak of personal achievement whose proof, whose trophy we carry off, in our hand, or in a bag, or on our bodies, as in the case of the Selfridges bikinis, the most spectacular catch of all, which we tied on over our underpants and bras, an accouterment that kept us wildly entertained all the way home on the Tube.

Our term for the audacity of going through with it was "nerve." To have the nerve gave one cause for pride and even inspired emulation.

As she pinches sweets from the Rabbits' tobacco shop, does Annie Duchesne see her parents in the pair of unsuspecting small shopkeepers whom she merrily fleeces in the company of R? Is she touched by anything resembling guilt? I do not think so, even if, today, the severe and lackluster face of Mrs. Rabbit tends to merge with that of my mother at the end of her life. The girl is in a state of moral amnesia, whereby the things that one does with another person elude our moral judgment. We would not have stolen a penny from anyone, and had we found a wallet full of bills on the street, we would have turned it in to the police. We did not think of ourselves as delinquents, but simply as girls who were more intrepid and *open-minded* than others.

Among the handful of poems I wrote a year later, I found this one, which begins:

> It was at Tottenham Court Road
> My face in the imperious mirror
> Glimmered with fear
> The teahouse fled toward the evening
> It was another world

Gray and cold as eternity.*

I remember asking friends at university to read it, no doubt proud to have transfigured a real, shameful episode into a mysterious, immaterial substance through a volley of metaphors. But because of this poem, perhaps, the image that prompted its writing was able to journey through time without being altered: that of a girl alone in a teahouse with mirrors all around her, seeing herself.

Not long before, at the exit of an Oxford Street department store, a hand had closed around an arm, the hand not mine but that of a short and strikingly ugly woman in a blue suit with a nose jutting out like a spike from the middle of her face. She forced R to follow her back inside the store and strictly forbade me to follow. A detective. In the Accessories section on the ground floor, where we'd decided by mutual agreement to go that day, I had been unable to steal anything, strangely ill at ease, somehow hindered. I said, frustrated by my inability to forage free of worry as R did, "I don't know what's wrong with me today, I don't have the nerve."

In that Tottenham teahouse, where I'd probably told R that I would wait for her, I see the girl alone at a table, in a brown fake suede jacket, watching the door, where finally the housewife who is R's employer will appear, alerted

* *C'était à Tottenham Court Road / Dans la glace impérieuse / Mon visage suintait la peur / Le tea-house filait vers le soir / C'était dans un autre monde / Gris et froid comme l'éternité.*

by the police. I wonder about the girl. Does she feel anything besides a kind of stupor—so it wasn't a game, after all—and the relief of having been spared by fate in some incomprehensible way, by some kind of miracle? Today I would simply attribute this to my peculiar sensitivity to the presence of others and their eyes upon me, a kind of permeability. Still one must suppose the girl is assailed by the conviction that her life has become a complete failure, though I don't know if she traces the failure back to the camp at S, as I will later.

R stood her ground, denied everything with aplomb, in spite of the pair of gloves and other trinkets found in her pockets. Her English family helped her avoid a night in jail by paying twenty pounds' bail. She appeared in court the following week and I testified to her innocence by swearing on the Bible—I must have made some progress with English by then—with the same determination I applied to taking an exam. The Portners thought I was *marvelous*. R's lawyer closed his argument by asking the court to look at the face of the accused—was it not the very image of innocence? He pointed to R's round face under her pixie cut (inspired by Jean Seberg in *Bonjour Tristesse*, which we had just seen), while propagating the certainty that the detective's mean and nasty face attested to the falsity of her accusations.

R was declared not guilty. Our escapade, which ended on a note of glory, had lasted two and a half months, all in all.

This call to order from a society that for us possessed no substance from a legal point of view, reduced now merely to its visual elements, punctured the playful bubble in which we lived. By summoning R to court and compelling me to take an oath, England was taking care of us, had helped bring home to us the meaning of our actions. As for our victory over the law, it made the whole thing easier to forget. Comparing what had happened with the worst that could befall a girl in 1960, R came to the right conclusion: It was better than getting pregnant. It seems to me that we very quickly ceased to talk about it. A shameful secret shared.

The last real image I have of R is that of an ungainly, joyless young woman in a yellow summer dress and blue cardigan walking away, down a path, with her husband and her little girl at the spa park of Saint-Honoré-les-Bains, and getting into a Citroën DS in the parking lot, one morning in late August 1971.

I do not know what has become of her: this ignorance, along with the time that has elapsed, have granted me permission to relate events that involve her. As if the girl R who vanished from my life over half a century ago no longer existed anywhere—or as if I denied she had any existence apart from the one she had with me. When I started to write about her, through a ruse of the unconscious, I continually put off questioning my right to unveil her. In a way, I blocked my scruples in order to attain the point where I am now, where I know it is impossible for me to remove—sacrifice—everything I have written about her up until now. This also applies to what I have written about myself. That is how this writing differs from a fictional narrative. There can be no tampering with reality, with the *this-happened* element, recorded in the archives of a London court, with our names: hers as the accused and mine as witness for the defense.

What flow of thoughts and memories, what subjective reality can I ascribe to the girl in the only photo I have of myself in England as an au pair, taken by R at the Finchley outdoor pool, a black-and-white photo, 2 by 2 inches, poorly framed and shot from a distance, which shows me sitting poolside on the pavement with a field and trees in the background? What could those thoughts have been if not the first intimations of what I would later become, or believed I was already.

A frothy blond updo, à la Brigitte Bardot; the blue bikini nicked from Selfridges, sunglasses, a studied pose—I lean back on one arm, stretched out behind me, the other arm limply draped over the folded legs—that sets off to their best advantage the slender waist and the obviously false bosom, produced by underwire and padding. I see a girl of the pinup type. Annie D has succeeded in becoming a larger version of the blonde from the summer camp of S, H's blonde. Except this is a cold, bulimic pinup girl who does not have periods and haughtily repels male advances. "At the pool, I spoke with three boys, a Swiss, an Austrian, and a German. They were funny, interesting, but I recoiled at their veiled suggestions and our relations went no further." Letter of August 18, 1960.

The entire memory of the camp has been walled up. The past of "a nothing girl," which the presence of R, "a real young lady," has caused her to repress. Forbidden to confide in R, I reinforce my forgetting. In her company, I quietly forge a sort of respectability. Whether or not she has lost her virginity from an anatomical point of view, the whore around the edges becomes "a real young lady." Who remembers the other girl now? Truly nobody.

Lying, eyes closed, on her bath towel, the girl in the photo feels (as I will write in a letter) "a thousand leagues away from my former self." I imagine her absorbed in images from childhood. For it is there, one afternoon in London, that the hum of an airplane in the sky took her back in time, with a kind of sweetness, to the war and the bombardments, the shriek of bomb alerts in the street. She sees her parents in a sort of separate love, from afar, old, kind, and slightly ridiculous, in their little shop. It's as if reality, of its own accord, were putting itself at a distance.

I started to make a literary being of myself, someone who lives as if her experiences were to be written down someday.

One Sunday afternoon in late August or early September 1960, I sit alone on a bench in a park near Woodside Park Station. The sun is shining. Children are playing. I have brought things to write with. I start a novel. I write a page or two, perhaps less. Maybe only this scene: A girl is lying on a bed with a man, she gets up and goes to the city.

All that remains of this beginning that has since disappeared is a distinct memory of the first sentence: Horses danced slowly by the sea.

At the Portners', I saw a scene on television that deeply stirred me, two trained horses moving around a beach on their hind legs in slow motion. With this image, I wanted to evoke sensations that accompany sex, the feeling of time slowing down, stretching out, a sense of being mired. If I can judge from the very short novel I wrote two years later, which proceeds from this opening scene, it is not the reality of my story with H that I wish to relate, it is a way not to be in the world, of not knowing how to be—something immense and hazy, which may explain why I did not continue writing in the following days. No doubt I postponed the writing of the novel to my future life as a student of literature (or philosophy—I was undecided, because of Simone de Beauvoir). R knew nothing of my intention to write. I was sure that she would go out of her way to demonstrate the folly of my ambition.

I wonder if in starting the present book I was not irrepressibly drawn by the image of Woodside Park, by the girl on a bench, as if everything that had happened since the night at the summer camp, one blunder after another, led up to this inaugural gesture. In which case, this would be the story of a perilous crossing to the harbor of writing, and, in the end, an uplifting demonstration of the fact that what counts is not the things that happen, but what we do with them. All this belongs to the realm of reassuring beliefs which are fated, as we age, to become more and more deeply ingrained in us, but whose truth is fundamentally impossible to establish.

In January 1989, I went to London for a weekend with several other writers for a literary event at the Barbican. On Sunday morning, when nothing else was scheduled, I took the Northern Line to East Finchley, then the bus, and asked the driver for the Granville Road stop, closest to the Portner house. Just before the bus stopped, I saw the swimming pool. I walked down Kenver Avenue. The Portners' house seemed quite small and ordinary. At Tally Ho Corner, only the Woolworth's remained. Rabbit Tobacconist was gone, as was the cinema, where a poster for *Suddenly, Last Summer* with Elizabeth Taylor had made me yearn to see the film (I would only see it ten years later), and where one could buy big bags of popcorn without going to the film. I took the Tube back to Woodside Park. I do not remember seeing the garden again. On my way home, I wrote in my journal: "All the conference participants made a beeline for the museums while I plunged back into my past life in North Finchley. I am not a culture hound, the only thing that matters to me is to seize life and time, understand, and take pleasure."

Is this the greatest truth of all in this story?

It is autumn, the beginning of October 1960. In a few days, I will take the boat for Dieppe with R, leave England, return to Yvetot, and enroll in my first year of undergraduate studies at the University of Rouen. The final letter from England reads: "After a year of idleness, I am back to work, and I am sure to find the change quite hard. But it is more pleasant to be occupied because one has a greater sense of being useful, of creating, if only school essays of no use whatsoever to society!"

I will commute between the grocery shop and the university, half an hour by express train or railcar. There is no girls' dorm at the university, and I refuse to endure the sadness of another residence hall run by nuns. The embarrassment my parents cause me—my father saying, "We was," my mother shouting at him, etc.—is not as strong as my need for the refuge they and their little shop provide—the refuge of childhood. In exchange, I will give them all of the scholarship money I was granted by the government—the maximum amount for me, the minimum for R.

In the lecture hall on the first day of school I am in a state of great excitement. I can't wait to go to the municipal library and borrow all the works whose titles have just been dictated by Professor Alexandre Micha, head of the department of literature. We write them down; the list is three pages long. I live in a constant state of intellectual effervescence, a happy effusiveness, waiting to meet new peers. In front of the bulletin board where the courses are posted, I strike up a conversation with G, who is pretty and very slender. We quickly become friends, and I notice that she eats almost nothing other than sweets and yogurt. I acquire a French national students' union card. The world and politics concern me.

I subscribe to *Lettres françaises*, edited by Louis Aragon, and Sunday morning I go to the Yvetot library to borrow books from the "new arrivals" shelf, Robbe-Grillet, Philippe Sollers. For my first essay in my practical work group, I received the highest grade. I attend the courses with a feeling of plenitude and pride. All the songs of that autumn, "*Âge tendre et tête de bois*," "Never on Sunday," "Green Fields," carry my happiness inside them.

I am making my way toward the book I will write, just as, two years earlier, I made my way toward love.

The obsession with food has left me, and my appetite has returned to what it was before the summer camp at S. My period returned at the end of October. I realize that this story is contained between two temporal boundaries related to food and blood, the boundaries of the body.

It seems to me that I'd stopped wondering whether I was a virgin. In my head I had become one again.

(In Seoul, in 1995, accompanied by a man from the embassy, I walked down alleys where working girls wait for customers behind windows next to charcoal heaters. The man said they came up from the country and returned a few years later, married, and forgot about what no one else knew.)

Letter of December 1961, to Marie-Claude:
"I've shut myself away, cloistered, trying to sit quietly alone in my room, as Pascal put it. My best moments are around five o'clock in the evening, when I watch the sun set through the window. The cold turns everything motionless outside, and I have just worked four hours without stopping. The poorly lit municipal library appeals to me, too. [. . .] there is this phrase by Nietzsche that I find so beautiful: We have Art in order not to die of the Truth."

In the summer of '62, the first summer after the end of the war in Algeria, I went on holiday with M, a friend from the university who had bought a 2cv with her salary as a primary school teacher. We went to Spain. I planned our route from Yvetot to the Spanish border, and also arranged for us to go by way of the Orne, near S. In the late morning, we arrived in the area of S, and I asked M if, as a favor, she would agree for us to stop at the sanatorium—the *aerium* where I had worked four years earlier. We were in no hurry, and she saw no reason not to, if it would make me happy. I guided her without difficulty. It was a shadowy road that seemed less familiar than I had thought. We parked in front of the entrance porch and I surveyed the scene from the car. The porter's lodgings on the right, the flower bed, supposedly pruned in the shape of a sleeveless sweater vest, the sanatorium's gray façade. No children or counselors in sight. I do not know why I did not get out of the 2cv— probably due to a fear of being recognized. It was early July, warm, overcast. I was wearing a navy blue suit—which was too hot, and which I would not put back on, once we had crossed the Loire—and a little candy-pink sweater. That is, I was dressed exactly like "the blonde" as she was on the first day, at the infirmary, when there were just the two of us, and we had our lungs X-rayed and urinated in jars.

I do not know quite what I felt at that precise moment of 1962, in the 2cv, whose window I had to roll up all the way to fill myself with the view of the place I had left four years before. To be aware of what I felt, I would have to know what memories crossed my mind, at that moment, of the weeks I had spent at S, to go back and find in what shifting, nebulous form my life of barely twenty-two years was present within me. It is possible that I felt nothing but the usual astonishment to find that the place did not match the image I retained of it. By wanting to return to the camp,

I was not trying to feel anything in particular, I was still too young to have that sort of desire—and I had not yet read all of *In Search of Lost Time*. I was coming back to show how different I was from the girl of '58, to assert my new identity—a bright and respectable student of literature, destined for the *agrégation** and writing—and assess the gap between the two. Fundamentally, I had not come back so that the places of '58 would "speak to me," but to tell the gray walls of the seventeenth-century building, and the little window of my room at the very top, under the eaves, that I no longer had anything to do with the girl of '58.

It also seems to me that I wanted to return to S and see the colony again because I hoped, in that way, to mine it for the energy to write the novel I wanted to begin. A kind of necessary precondition, beneficial to writing, a kind of propitiatory gesture—the first in a series that will later take me back to a variety of places—or a kind of prayer, as if the place were able to act as an obscure intermediary between past reality and writing. Basically, the detour via S was akin to the kiss which, after waiting my turn in a line of pilgrims, and to the great disgust of M (who refrained) I planted on the foot of the black Virgin of Monserrat, while making the wish to write a novel.

I wrote it in the fall, a very short text I titled *The Tree*, after a phrase read in Mérimée's *Correspondence*: "We must

---

* The highest teaching diploma in France.

get used to living like a tree." Later, after its rejection by Éditions du Seuil, I changed the title to *The Five O'Clock Sun* and sent it to Buchet-Chastel, who rejected it, too.

In the summer of 1963, when I was twenty-three, in the wood-ceilinged room of a small hotel-restaurant in Saint-Hilaire-du-Touvet, Chez Jacques, my anatomical virginity was proven beyond a shadow of a doubt. I only knew the boy's first name, Philippe. In the first letter he wrote me, I learned his last name was Ernaux, and was disturbed by its similarity with the word "Ernemont." According to what I could remember of linguistics, these first three letters attested to a shared Germanic origin, in which I saw a mysterious sign.

I have moved ahead in the writing of this text without looking back.

It occurs to me that it all could have been written in another way, as a statement of raw fact, for example. Or based on particular details: the bar of soap from the first night, the words written in red toothpaste on the mirror, the closed door of the second night, the jukebox that played "Apache" in the coffee shop of Tally Ho Corner, the name Paul Anka deeply engraved on a desk at the lycée, the 45 rpm of "Only You," bought with R at a record store after we had listened to it together in a booth, and which I played on Saturday night with the lights off, slow-dancing alone in my room in Yvetot.

It is the absence of meaning in what one lives, at the moment one lives it, which multiplies the possibilities of writing.

The memory of what I have written is already fading. I do not know what this piece of writing is. Even the thing I was pursuing by writing this book has dissolved. Among my papers I found a sort of note of intent:

Explore the gulf between the stupefying reality of things that happen, at the moment they happen, and, years later, the strange unreality in which the things that happened are enveloped.

The author of some twenty works of fiction and memoir, ANNIE ERNAUX is considered by many to be France's most important literary voice. She won the Prix Renaudot for *A Man's Place* and the Marguerite Yourcenar Prize for her body of work. More recently she received the International Strega Prize, the Prix Formentor, and the French-American Translation Prize for *The Years*, which was also shortlisted for the Man Booker International Prize and the Warwick Prize for Women in Translation.

ALISON L. STRAYER is a Canadian writer and translator. Her work has been shortlisted for the Governor General's Award for Literature and for Translation, the Grand Prix du livre de Montreal, the Prix littéraire France-Québec, the Warwick Prize for Women in Translation, and the Man Booker International Prize. She lives in Paris.

About Seven Stories Press

SEVEN STORIES PRESS is an independent book publisher based in New York City. We publish works of the imagination by such writers as Nelson Algren, Russell Banks, Octavia E. Butler, Ani DiFranco, Assia Djebar, Ariel Dorfman, Coco Fusco, Barry Gifford, Martha Long, Luis Negrón, Hwang Sok-yong, Lee Stringer, and Kurt Vonnegut, to name a few, together with political titles by voices of conscience, including Subhankar Banerjee, the Boston Women's Health Collective, Noam Chomsky, Angela Y. Davis, Human Rights Watch, Derrick Jensen, Ralph Nader, Loretta Napoleoni, Gary Null, Greg Palast, Project Censored, Barbara Seaman, Alice Walker, Gary Webb, and Howard Zinn, among many others. Seven Stories Press believes publishers have a special responsibility to defend free speech and human rights, and to celebrate the gifts of the human imagination, wherever we can. In 2012 we launched Triangle Square books for young readers with strong social justice and narrative components, telling personal stories of courage and commitment. For additional information, visit www.sevenstories.com.